The Strangled Impulse

WILLIAM KING

THE LILLIPUT PRESS

DUBLIN

COMHAIRLE CHONTAE ÁTHA CLIATH THEAS
SOUTH DUBLIN COUNTY LIBRARIES

COUNTY LIBRARY, TOWN CENTRE, TALLAGHT
TO RENEW ANY ITEM TEL: 462 0073
OR ONLINE AT www.southdublinlibraries.ie

Items should be returned on or before the last date below. Fines, as displayed in the Library, will be charged on overdue items.

Published in 2014 by
The Lilliput Press,
62-63 Sitric Road,
Dublin 7, Ireland
www.lilliputpress.ie

ISBN: 978 1 84351 6217

A cip record for this title is available from The British Library.

10 9 8 7 6 5 4 3 2 1

Typeset by Linden Publishing Services in 11 on 13 point Bembo
Designed by Susan Waine
Printed in Poland by Bookpress.eu, ul. Struga 2, Olsztyn 10-270

'For the strangled impulse there is no redemption.'
PATRICK KAVANAGH, *The Great Hunger*

One

A time-honoured custom in the diocese obliged all curates who had received a letter of appointment from the bishop to introduce themselves to their new superiors. But like someone putting off a visit to the doctor because he fears the worst, Brian O'Neill deferred, for as long as he could, the courtesy call on Father Leo Brannigan, parish priest of Melrose. What he had heard about Brannigan caused him to postpone even further the inevitable moment. Nevertheless, about three or four days after receiving the galling missive, he rang.

'I have found Melrose on the map but I'm not sure how to get there,' he told the parish priest.

'You don't need any map. It couldn't be simpler.' He seemed irritated. 'Turn off the Swords Road at the signpost for the new hospital, right at the Maxol station and left at The Spanish Lady. You're on your way to Melrose then. You can't miss it.'

But he did. An articulated truck coming towards him obstructed his view of the signpost and he was heading for the airport before he realized his mistake. Eventually he found Melrose and the church, a giant bird that had spread its wings and landed on the green space at the centre of the estate. Across the road, three fellows with shaven heads stood outside a newsagent's. He stopped and lowered the window.

'Excuse me, lads,' he called. An Alsatian barked and strained at the chain. Hooded eyes sized him up. 'Can you tell me where the parish priest's house is?' Two of them were leaning against the defaced brick wall; the third, holding the dog, kept his back to him.

'Beano,' said one, 'you know where the parish priest's house is?'

'I do in me bollix.'

His back still half-turned to the road, Beano shouted across: 'Go around by the Grove and then somewhere up in Greenoaks, in the purchase houses.'

The others jeered him.

'Will youse fuck up while I'm tellin' the bloke the way.'

'Thanks,' said Brian, winding up the window.

A big woman with jet-black hair, grey at the roots, half-opened the door of the parochial house.

'Yes?' She glared at him through thick lenses.

'I'm here to see Father Brannigan.'

'He can't see you now. He has another appointment.' She couldn't see his collar beneath the scarf.

'I'm Father O'Neill.' He returned her stare.

She burst into a fit of laughter that became a bronchial cough. 'And why didn't you say so in the first place? Come in before I catch my death.'

Her handshake was indifferent. In the hallway, she knocked on a door, and, without waiting for an answer, swaggered off towards the kitchen.

Father Brannigan removed his reading glasses. 'I was trying to get the accounts ready for the auditor. Hang your coat there.'

He pointed to the metal rack behind the door. Propped against the corner was a set of golf clubs, blades of grass stuck to one of the steel heads.

The pier glass mirrored the two men: beside Father Brannigan's craggy features and wide girth, Brian looked straight out of the seminary.

The parish priest led the way into the sitting room, motioned with his hand to one of the fireside chairs and resumed his seat behind a desk, littered with newspaper cuttings and old books.

One section of a Superser glowed red, filling the air with a gaseous smell. Over the mantelpiece was a faded photograph, cameos of young priests, at the centre a frontal view of All Saints Seminary. The inscription underneath read: Ordination Day, June 1948.

The two priests took soundings with neutral topics: the cold weather, the journey over, and how the city was expanding.

'Very soon,' said Father Brannigan, 'when they build the new road to the airport, it will be much quicker. European Community funds, you know, money no object.'

Brian nodded to the florid profile. He relaxed and crossed his legs. Father Brannigan, too, felt more at ease. His informants were right: Brian O'Neill wouldn't cause him any bother.

The conversation strayed to Beechmount. The parish priest knew the place well; once, he had been a curate in Blackrock. 'Three of us and the Canon, and in the eight years we worked for him, he never had an ounce of trouble from us.'

He began to tap the desk with his fingers.

'I'm sure you're anxious to see where you'll be living. Give me a minute to get the keys. Not exactly what you've been used to in Beechmount though.'

Brian was free now to survey the room. On a card table beside him were thin batches of typescript. The title-page, *Men of the Harvest*, in heavy black print with the parish priest's name beneath, lay on top of one batch.

'All ready for the publishers.' When he came back in, Father Brannigan spotted the sideways look and seized the opportunity. He picked up one of the batches and flicked through the pages.

'The men who built this diocese. God be good to them.' His hurry forgotten, he recalled moments from the proud record.

'By the way,' he addressed the card table: 'Have you seen my other books?'

'Yes. I have.'

Father Brannigan's fixation with writing rose-tinted histories of the Church was well known; one or two of these he had succeeded in getting published in pamphlet form. They were displayed, dog-eared and faded, on church bookstalls throughout the diocese.

On the way to show the new church to his curate, Father Brannigan tapped the steering wheel while he gave a potted account of the parish. When they reached the open space, he pointed towards the squat structure: 'I was given a green field and told to build on that.' He rattled off figures about bank charges and the current state of the debt and repeated the amount he had collected since he had founded the parish.

The three skinheads still loitered in front of the newsagent's; a small child playing near a pool of water aimed a pebble at the car. Keeping his gaze fixed straight ahead, the parish priest wheeled into the church grounds: 'Would you look.' He made jabbing angry movements with his thumb. 'If only there was conscription; that would put manners on them.'

At the door of the church he resumed his commentary. He disagreed with the open plan, over which he swept a huge hand, but the architect felt it suited that type of building. 'He doesn't have to clear those brats who use the lower part of the roof as a slide during the summer holidays, and if I had my way, I'd have put up a good high fence all around.'

Someone had told him recently about a solution called 'Non Climb' and he was going to apply that to the down-pipes. 'Sticky stuff,' he gloated, 'that will cause a nice mess to their clothes if they attempt to go on the roof.'

Across the road, children were yelling and chasing each other around the school playground. A severe-looking man appeared at the main door, ringing a bell for all he was worth and shouting: '*Líne díreach. Líne díreach.*'

'That's Muredach Hogan,' the parish priest said, 'the principal of Holy Trinity. Very loyal to the Church.'

While listening to an account of the principal's virtues, Brian kept his eyes on the lean figure, wagging his finger at a child who had stepped out of line.

Father Brannigan rattled the keys, shifting from one foot to the other.

'The school behind is Divine Grace. Bill Sweeney is the principal there, he's due for retirement in June.' They could see over the flat roof and the skylights a building identical to the one inside the railing.

The parish priest pointed towards a row of semi-detached houses that stretched down from Greenoaks, a residential area, kept at arm's length from the dull grey and brown of the corporation estate by Melrose Road.

'Your house is over there in Greenoaks Lawn. Dick Hegarty, the senior curate, is beside you. And away up there is Davis Towers, which you've probably heard of. Say no more.' Lines of washing fell limp over the balconies of the two high-rise blocks.

Inside the church, the parish priest stressed the special features: the seating formation and the roof light above the altar. Though he nodded and made appreciative sounds, Brian was unimpressed with the Church of the Resurrection. The naked walls and the network of steel girders suggested the word 'factory' to his mind: a far cry from the stained-glass and marble splendour he was leaving.

The tour over, both men went across the green by a narrow footpath to the curate's house. A yellow skip squatting in front of the garage door left just enough space for one to squeeze through the gateway. Father Brannigan went ahead and opened the door to a foul smell that rose from the carpet; he went straight through to the kitchen where the reek of grease hung in the air.

'The windows should have been opened,' he muttered, his feet sounding hollow on the linoleum. Around the rings of the cooker were brown stains; dried grease streaked the door as if it had oozed from the grill.

'Liam Holden, your predecessor, wasn't much of a housekeeper,' he explained when he noticed Brian looking at the broken tiles from the fireplace strewn on the carpet of the living room. The grate was littered with cigarette butts, a calendar of the previous year showing the month of August hung on the back of the door.

Upstairs was much the same. The chrome handle for flushing the toilet lay on the windowsill and a piece of cord was tied to the exposed cistern. Here also a sickening smell polluted the air.

In the box room a mouse scurried along the skirting board and disappeared into a mass of newspapers banked up against the wall.

'One of Liam's projects.' The parish priest threw a baleful glance towards the mound. 'Supposed to be for the missions. Recycled paper.' He shook his head in contempt.

'It won't be too bad when you get a bit of spring cleaning

done. Houses always look desolate when they're empty,' was his parting remark at the front gate of his house.

Like a flint spark, the remark fired the anger that smouldered after Brian had seen where he would be living. Yet he held himself in check. A quarrel now would poison for ever any hope of peace in the future; however, he couldn't let it pass. 'There are a few things to be done. I mean the bathroom isn't in great shape.' He was wary.

'We'll see.' The hand shot up and the fingers raked through the silver mop. 'Maybe a good wash down would do. There are a few women in the parish who would do that if you wanted them. I could organize it. We'll see.'

Before he returned to Beechmount, Brian cruised along by the flat-roofed row of empty shops where he had asked directions. He stopped to take a closer look. Each unit was a dark cave. Graffiti on the supporting pillars added to the squalor: 'Bob Marley RIP.' and 'Guards is bastards.'

In one den a fire was burning and young people were huddled around it; they sat on milk crates, poking the fire with sticks. One of them cast a sullen glance at him and then turned away.

On the way out of the estate, he again lost his bearings but continued past the tower blocks, searching for a landmark. A shopping trolley lay capsized in a pond of water and from across an open green came the thud of hooves. He had to brake sharply to avoid two boys on ponies; they raced in front and cantered on beside him on the footpath. Every time they dug their heels into the ponies' sides, steam rose from the animals' sweat-drenched flanks and they set off at a gallop, laughing and shouting at each other.

Back in Beechmount, he kept himself busy packing and saying goodbye to parishioners, living as far as possible from the rupture to his life. Waves of resentment attacked his defences, but he took shelter in the prescription handed out in the seminary: the will of God is expressed through the lawful authority of the Church. He made out a programme for the remaining days: a reflex action, characteristic of a man who had always immersed himself in parish work whenever clouds threatened his horizon. Apart from his day off, every hour was accounted for with committees, groups and projects of one kind or another.

He was filling the old trunk he had had since his days in St Bernard's boarding school when Paul Duggan called one evening.

'I got your message late, Brian,' he explained in the hallway. 'I was delayed in the hospital that night.'

'That's okay. Maybe it's just as well, considering the mood I was in.'

The evening he had received the archbishop's letter, he had rung his friend several times, holding on longer on each occasion. Then he phoned the housekeeper in the basement of the old presbytery. 'Father Duggan is at the hospital and he won't be back,' she rasped above the theme music from *Dallas*.

While Brian poured a gin and tonic, and a whiskey for himself, Paul glanced at the fresh patches where the pictures had hung. At one end of the sitting room an assortment of cardboard boxes was heaped; one of the high doors leading to the dining room was open, revealing books and tea chests piled beside the mahogany table.

'What's going to happen to your Parish Renewal programme?' Paul asked.

'It will probably go the way of many another project that priests have to put aside when the Boss, as they call him, blows full-time.'

He picked up a hardcover copybook from the table. 'Three years of planning and going around to houses and drinking cups of tea that I didn't want, and holding meetings here in this room and now ....' He held the copybook over the wickerwork basket and let it drop.

'Maybe you'll be able to do something with it in that place you're going to.'

'From what I saw of Davis Towers and Melrose,' he gave a scornful laugh, 'I wouldn't imagine that parish renewal is very high on their list of priorities.'

He raised himself from the armchair and took down a folded sheet from the mantelpiece. 'Listen to this:

Dear Father O'Neill,
I have pleasure in appointing you to the parish of the Resurrection, Melrose, with effect from Saturday, 12 February.

You will be replacing Father Liam Holden CC. Please contact Father Leo Brannigan, Parish Priest, in order to make the necessary arrangements.

May I take this opportunity to thank you for the work you have done in Beechmount and to wish you every blessing in the future. Sincerely in Christ,
+Joseph.'

He folded the letter and returned it to the stone mantel.

'The twelfth.' Paul took a diary from his inside pocket. 'That's tomorrow week. Of all Saturdays.' He looked away. 'I can't help you to move out. There's a conference for chaplains in the hospital and if I missed it, there would be war. Sorry about that.'

'Not to worry.' Brian suppressed his disappointment. 'Anyway, I've most of the packing done and I've hired a transport company for the removal.'

But when his friend had gone, the full impact of leaving on his own, and before his parish project had seen the light of day, collided with his brave effort to suppress his frustration. Curiously an image from childhood came to him of a day out in Ballybunion. He had just completed the perfect sandcastle when his brother, Donal, four years older and about to cross the line into adolescence, bounded over the strand and charged through his work of art. Before him lay his toil in a sandy ruin and all he could do was sit back on his heels and suffer the hoots of laughter and the strong legs threshing up the surf.

On his last day in Beechmount, Tim Sheridan, his parish priest, dropped in on his way to visit the school. As he paced along the wide hallway, sometimes running his hand along the wainscotting, he had a flow of advice: 'Watch those removals men in case they damage your furniture. Do no work for about three weeks or a month until you've sized up the place, and don't take any nonsense from Brannigan. His bark is worse than his bite.' The chatter was a cover-up for his feelings. On the previous Monday night, after a few drinks in his house with the men who counted the Sunday collection, tears had welled up in the parish priest's eyes and he had blurted out: 'The son I never had.' His hearers dodged the awkward moment with a show of interest in the television screen.

He was now sidling to the door: 'Well, I thought you'd be with us for another year, but that's the way. Ours is not to reason why.' He removed his glasses and scrutinized a batch of letters.

'I've something for you.' He handed him a bulky envelope and shook his hand: 'You're a good priest and if you have faults – in someone else they would be virtues.'

'Thanks, Tim, thanks for everything.' To escape from an uprush of sadness, he began to examine the foot scraper as if seeing it for the first time. He waited while the other man, remarkably nimble for his years, tripped down the steps. Brian stood there, until the car was out of sight, then sauntered back in, examining the envelope as he closed the heavy door behind him. In the sitting room, he counted out one hundred and fifty pounds.

When everyone had gone that night, he was restless. He moped about from the dining room to the kitchen, checking that the boxes were ready and labelled. The skeletal remains of his house already belonged to his successor, who had come one day with his mother, a woman with thin lips; she planned where bookcases and wardrobes would go: he used the measuring tape and she recorded the particulars in a notebook.

The naked light bulb cast a deserted look on the big living room, bare except for the one armchair on its own before the television. At the other end was a heap of presents he thought best to take in the car: two silver salvers, crystal-cut wine glasses, a set of golf clubs, a Persian rug and a bone-china tea set. From nowhere came a wild impulse to aim a kick at the pile and send crystal and silver flying. Instead, as he turned to the armchair, his eye fell on the bottle of whiskey and an open pack of Club Orange left over after treating his visitors. He poured a double measure of Jameson and slumped into the chair.

Save for the trickle of water through the radiators or the occasional creak somewhere in the roof, the house was silent. He longed for company and wished the Byrnes hadn't left so early, but they had tickets for the National Concert Hall.

He cast an eye about the room. Tomorrow his successor and his mother would move in. At least she wouldn't have any vacumming to do; the girls had seen to that.

Elaine Curran and Lorna Clarke, who were sitting for their Leaving Certificate in Nagle House School the following June, had been coming to the presbytery since they were First Years. The arrangement suited everyone: they had peace to do their homework and the priest had someone to take phone calls while he was out around the parish.

The same Elaine had flowered into a beautiful woman; already her youth and vigour were stretching the green uniform. Her skin had a glow of health the evening she had called to discuss a serious problem: she was losing her faith and he was the only one who could help her. He had hardly begun to reassure her that most people experience the growing pains of doubt when she shed her distress. She was full of questions: why can't priests marry? Why did he become a priest?

He reached for the remote control and switched from one channel to another and then back to hear a summary of the news. A soldier had been shot in Strabane; the Minister for Finance was warning of higher inflation rates because of foreign borrowings; more frost was forecast for the night and the following day, then milder weather with strong winds for Sunday. He shot dead the picture and sat staring at the grey screen until his own sullen face looked out at him.

Again he wandered about the room and refilled the whiskey glass. As he poured, his thoughts drifted to what the parish priest had said that evening after they had celebrated the seven-thirty Mass together: 'I remember when I was a young curate – around your age. I got notice on the Monday to be in Rathdrum for confessions on Saturday night. The day before, the archbishop had been in the parish for Confirmation; do you think he would even hint at it?' His mouth twisted in a cynical grin, 'I'm afraid you and I don't count when the powers-that-be start to play chess.'

Two

Long before dawn, Brian cleared the garden shed of waste: an old pair of football boots, a sombrero he had brought from California, several pairs of shoes and the guitar he had had in All Saints, the shaft held to the body by three strings.

Orange brush strokes were streaking the sky over Dún Laoghaire when he threw the last of the plastic bags on top of the hired skip. The grassy embankment, which sloped upwards from the edge of the yard towards the surrounding hedge, had become a pincushion of needles overnight and the remains of the previous day's snowfall lay along the kerbstone. From the direction of the shops came the rattle of a steel shutter; the rasping sound vibrated in the chill air.

He worked on in the walled garden until he heard the crunch of tyres on the gravel and the squeak of brakes. Then, through the open gateway, he saw a man about his own age in beige overalls directing the lorry driver to the foot of the steps.

Though well-practised at steering a course around corners with heavy furniture, they had difficulty with the piano. Brian stayed with them until they had it safely in the truck, then he returned to the garden to collect a few plants. Their contented small talk reached him while he worked.

'And we're off to Killarney this evenin' until Sunday night. There's a special fare durin' the off-season. Yourself and Rose should try it sometime.'

'We might an' all. It would be no harm to get her out of the house for a while.'

'I'm not jokin' you, Anto, but you should see the meals they put up. Ah, I guarantee you'd never finish them.' He hesitated: 'I can't remember the name of the hotel. Bernie looks after all that. Me an' her go every year. For the anniversary.'

A blip sounded in Brian's head: he saw them at their ease in a restaurant, sharing a private language and savouring the pleasures of the night ahead. The flow of conversation rubbed salt into the wound of his upheaval. And like someone in his sickbed who listens to the coming and going of the outside world, he felt cut off and alone.

The night before, images of what he had seen in Melrose and the house he would occupy sapped his energy, yet he was too restless to gain any more than fitful sleep. Thoughts of moving on his own made him worse.

When they arrived at his new address, he went ahead of the men and, bracing himself for the stench, turned the key in the door. The smell of fresh paint, when he stepped into the hallway, surprised him. He made a quick inspection of the house. The two rooms on the ground floor and one bedroom upstairs had been wallpapered; between the ceramic tiles around the fireplace, the grout was still drying out.

Their work was harder this time: they had to haul the massive wardrobe up the narrow stairs, and the confined space of the hallway restricted their movements.

By midday, however, the house was habitable, even if books and delph lay in boxes in the kitchen; more boxes and tea chests lay along the dining-room wall.

'I don't envy your job, Father.' The driver swept a forefinger over the collection while the priest wrote out a cheque. The younger man idly picked up a chess piece and studied it.

'Do you mind me askin' you, Father; do you have a say in where you are sent?'

Brian looked at the chess piece. 'Not much.'

'A bit like the army, Father.'

'A lot like the army.'

He stood at the door until the lorry was out of sight, then, before he went in, scanned the foreign skyline: clouds, the colour of pewter, threatened the tower blocks; across the green on the wide concrete leading to the church, children raced up and down on roller skates; a gust of wind lifted a Dunnes Stores bag, whipped it across the road and slapped it against the school railing. The forecast that he had heard, in what now seemed a far off country, was right: rain and strong winds to follow the frost. In the distance an ice-cream van struck up its rallying call, 'The Teddy Bears' Picnic'.

The house was perishing, so he switched on the central heating and busied himself in the kitchen putting cutlery in drawers, cleaning out shelves and stowing away delph. After a while he checked the radiators; they were stone cold. In the back yard the needle on the tank pointed to zero. He pulled shut the wooden gate at the side and was about to go in, when he heard his name being called.

'Are you getting settled in all right?' Father Dick Hegarty, the curate from next door, threw his leg over the low dividing wall. His broad smile recalled for Brian chance meetings at priests' conferences and the annual retreat at All Saints.

'It never rains but it pours, Dick. Looks like the tank is empty.'

'I'll lend you a Superser if you're stuck.'

'Thanks, but I should be able to manage. I've a couple of convectors; they'll get me through until Monday.'

'Come in for a cup of coffee anyway, and you're welcome to the parish. I missed you the day you called.' His handshake was friendly.

'Liam,' he said out of the corner of his mouth, 'used a Superser for the past couple of months, he didn't want to get a fill once he'd decided to bail out, afraid the replacement mightn't cough up.' When he smiled, his twinkling eyes narrowed into slits.

'Dympna,' he called in the hallway, and a pale-faced woman appeared. Over her skirt she wore a striped apron tied around her thickening waist. 'This is our new neighbour. Father O'Neill.'

Brian made to approach her, but she held up her yellow gloves. 'Can't shake hands.' She threw him a frosty glance. In a deferential tone, Father Hegarty asked her if she wouldn't mind making them coffee.

The two priests chatted about where they had ministered.

Melrose was Hegarty's sixth appointment. 'So in another five years I can expect my own parish.' He reached for a biscuit. 'There are twenty-four guys ahead of me, but with a bit of luck one or two might keel over in the meantime.' Again the eyes became slits. 'What about yourself?'

'This is my third move. Eight years in Beechmount and before that the usual stint in the Tech.'

'You're only a *garsún*.'

'I feel much older than a *garsún* for the past couple of days.'

'You'll get on fine here. It isn't a difficult parish, except for Davis-bloody-Towers. They think the world owes them a living. Shaggers need to get off their arses and do a day's work. Did you see what the gurriers did to the few shops? When I came here, that was a grand little place; there was a shop in each unit – you know, the usual.' He listed them off on his fingers: 'A butcher, a greengrocer, even a small supermarket. They wreck the schools too when they're mad with cider. Two of them broke in one evening when a teacher, Niamh Kirwan, and her trainee were putting up charts. I believe the trainee ran, but your woman picked up a blackboard pointer, and if either of them had got it where she jabbed, their marriage prospects wouldn't be very promising.'

'Brave woman,' Brian affected interest.

Dick's manner became confidential. 'I see Leo got the house done.' Again the habitual caution returned and he spoke in an undertone: 'Leo is okay; hates to fork out, though.' He was warming to his topic, but the phone cut him short. His smile vanished.

'Yes, you did a great job on that letter. Yes, if they don't get the message now they never will and it won't be your fault.' He listened. 'Yes, in fact he's here with me now.' Dick glanced at Brian, threw his eyes upwards and shaped a silent 'Leo' with his lips. 'Good, that's fine, Leo, you'll drop down, great. See you in a few minutes.'

He put down the phone: 'The Ayatollah is on his way.'

Father Brannigan didn't waste any time getting down to business. He used the briefcase on his knees as a desk and handed a typed sheet to his two curates.

'A list of duties,' he explained. 'I've included the Mass rota and the baptisms for the next six months. That should keep us going for a while.'

'As you know,' the parish priest said, eyes fixed on his desk, 'most men of my age don't do a day's duty, but I always believed in doing my share.'

'Yes,' Father Hegarty rushed to second the proud boast, 'no one could ever say that Leo doesn't do his part.'

Finally Father Brannigan handed Brian the *Status Animarum*: notebooks that contained a list of all the parishioners. 'These might help you when you are visiting Liam's area of the parish. At least the area he was supposed to visit.'

'Poor Liam slackened up on the visitation in the last couple of years,' Dick remarked. 'Probably shyness.'

The parish priest's fingers had begun to tap an urgent rhythm. 'You're being very kind. However,' he snapped shut the briefcase, 'we won't scandalize the new member of our team.'

Brian had a wedding in Trinity College Chapel the following Tuesday. The couple had met through the folk group and used to sing at Beechmount Church until they left home to take rooms in the college.

'Even if you are not in the parish, we want you to marry us,' they stressed when he had attended the engagement party at the bride's home.

Chandeliers glittered with rainbow colours when her father stood to deliver his speech at the reception in the Shelbourne. 'Many of you will know,' he said, turning to Brian, 'that a modest man among us has unconsciously played the part of cupid in the happy alliance we celebrate today.' A polite chuckle passed through the dining room. 'And,' he emphasized, 'I am reliably informed that the Folk Mass founded by Father O'Neill has become the catalyst for two other joyful unions to date.'

He inserted a thumb into a front pocket of his waistcoat: a court-room mannerism familiar to the junior members of his legal firm, some of whom were present at the wedding. He was pleased to announce a second cause for celebration: the day before, his new son-in-law had received a travelling scholarship to the Mayo Clinic. A cricket-match applause and 'Well done!' greeted his announcement.

Later in the ballroom, Brian mingled with his former parishioners. One glass of brandy after another was placed in his hand between dances, so that he lost track of time until he found himself with the others in a circle around the couple, now dressed for going away. After many promises that he would certainly take up their dinner invitations, he left unnoticed by the side door that opened onto Kildare Street.

Against a wall of O'Donoghue's pub, a couple, oblivious to the world, were wrapped around each other. He hurried to his car. Images from the evening, however, shadowed him: fingers easing the wedding ring into place and looks that promised fidelity, 'all the days of our lives'.

The following days he forced himself to open the boxes that were still lying in the hallway and the kitchen. The spare room became his library: here he arranged his books on adjustable shelving; the remainder he placed in the leaded glass case. On the wall over his desk he placed a print of Caravaggio's *Supper at Emmaus*, Tim Sheridan's present from a holiday in Milan. Last of all he hung the pictures, including a black and white photograph of St Bernard's College team the year they won the *Corn na Mumhain*. After a final touch to straighten the frame, he lingered over the faces: a younger Brian O'Neill with arms folded smiled at him from the back row.

While he worked or just wandered about the house, the hours were punctuated by the playground sounds from Holy Trinity; soon he could tell the time from the school's schedule: the short break at ten-thirty, then the half-hour at twelve o'clock and finally the cries of freedom at two-thirty. There was silence then except for Mr Whippy's ice-cream van or the rattle of skates in front of the church; at times too the rise and fade of a car engine on Melrose Road touched the edge of his consciousness.

He was determined to settle in and keep the sudden up-rooting at bay, so he began to draw up a programme in order to silence the inner voices of discontent. There was no reason, he assured himself, why he shouldn't adapt to his new parish after a few months; the people he had met outside the church on a Sunday seemed friendly. It was just a question of getting used to the place. The logic, however, was not able to muffle the faint drumbeat of gloom mingled with anger that persisted in his brain. But that too would disappear as soon as he got involved in parish work; remaining in the house was only making the situation worse.

Three

Thursday was his day off. Ever since Paul Duggan had joined the diocese, the two men had met regularly for golf. If the weather was too bad, they went to the pictures and had a meal afterwards. About once a month they played a four-ball with two others from Brian's ordination year, Philip Lynsky and Jude Looby.

After his sudden transfer from Wicklow, Looby turned up one day at Royal Dublin. 'Another Lynsky project and the fact that Looby is in Iggy Somers' parish could mean a lift up the greasy pole,' Paul remarked as they were driving home.

Neither of them trusted Lynsky. Behind the carefree manner, they sensed a craving for preferment. Sent to Rome after ordination, he had returned to be appointed to the staff of All Saints where he was an instant success with all the students. 'They see me as one of themselves, rather than as a member of the staff,' he boasted. But the popularity soon waned when they found that he withdrew at the last moment from their confrontation with the archbishop about college restrictions.

As expected, Brian's appointment was the topic for discussion on the Thursday after he had moved to Melrose. Paul and he were fitting on their rainwear when Looby, hunched under the weight of his golf bag, burst into the locker room ahead of Lynsky.

'No better man than yourself, Brian, to assist Leo with his next publication. Am I right, Paul?' Looby threw his bag on the low stool the golfers used for changing their shoes. 'Did he tell you that he should have been professor in All Saints, instead of being stuck in a dump?'

'No.'

'According to Leo, the man who was appointed had a vicar general for an uncle, but he himself received higher marks in Rome. Forty years ago and it still bothers him.' The voice broke into a girlish laugh. 'I knew you were on your way a week before you got the letter.'

'Somers?'

'I don't as a rule reveal my source, but since you guys are my nearest and dearest ....'

Monsignor Ignatius Somers, his informant, was on the personnel board that advised the archbishop about the deployment of priests. A little man who doused himself with aftershave, he was one of a group who phoned each other early in the morning with the latest piece of gossip. They knew if a priest was going to leave: who was dying and who would succeed to the vacancy. Somers made regular visits to Rome and had been influential in the appointment of at least two bishops. Looby had been the Monsignor's curate for five years. They went for walks together in Phoenix Park or the Botanic Gardens, and collogued over the breakfast table when the other priests had left. Through his golfing friend, Lynsky secured invitations to Somers' dinner parties.

On their way out by the gravelled path that led to the first tee, they could hear familiar voices in the distance and an unmistakable laugh.

'Your man is at it already, lads. Do you hear him?' Lynsky remarked. The priest he referred to had an endless succession of lewd jokes, and his guffaw, more like a bray, was a constant of the golfing day and had become a clarion that all was well in the clerical world.

At the back of the clubhouse they climbed the knoll that overlooked the course. Over to their left, three priests were waiting while a fourth was studying his approach. After some concentration and practice swings, he whacked the ball, which rose into the air, shot down the fairway and landed a short distance from the green. The others applauded. 'You're still able to get it up, Jim,' one of them said.

'Oh, yeah, Jim was always able to get it up.' The muffled reply caused an outburst of laughter.

One evening in the bar, Jim had provided Brian and Paul with gratuitous advice: 'You lads are much younger than us, but I'll tell you something that may be worth remembering: priests would be a lot more content if they got out and played golf, instead of chasing after skirts.' His friend reinforced the counsel. 'You notice, Paul. The guys who play golf never leave.'

Some of the priests, especially in summer, played golf two or three times a week, but Tuesday and Thursday were immovable feasts throughout the year. 'Royal Dublin on Tuesday, Milltown on Thursday,' had become a diocesan slogan.

When the four priests moved off, Lynsky and Paul led the way to the first tee. Any chance he got, Looby edged up to Brian.

'And tell me,' he asked, 'how is Dick getting on? Is he still looking around corners to see if anyone is after him?'

Brian ignored the comment with a chuckle. 'Seems fine so far, Jude.'

'Have you met Dympna?' The eyes behind the rimless glasses were hungry for scraps.

'The evening I arrived, but I haven't seen her much since.' On purpose, he didn't tell him that her car was in the driveway most days.

'She's been in tow since he was in Chapelizod.' Looby was bursting with the story. Soon after her husband had died, Dympna came for help to Father Hegarty. She couldn't sleep at night and even God had vanished from her life. She had complained of loneliness to another priest and how she missed the comforting arm of her late husband. 'Go over to the church and cuddle up to Jesus,' that man had told her.

Father Hegarty was different. He had invited her to come back again and talk whenever she felt depressed. By the time he was appointed to Melrose, they were going on holidays together, and taking her teenage daughter with them. When Hegarty's mother died, Dympna inherited her fur coat.

After the game, Brian and Paul parted with the other two priests and drove back into town. *The Woman in Red* was the only film worth going to and they'd already seen it, so they decided they would amble around to Neary's for a drink after their meal.

In the restaurant, Paul, who had been unusually quiet all day, now became voluble and launched into a sudden attack on the Church, lashing out about the Pope and how he was back in the dark ages.

'Do you know that in Rome there's a witch hunt in the seminaries? Theologians are looking over their shoulders, not knowing when they will be called by one of the Pope's lackeys to give an account of something they may have said in a lecture. Then you have young guys strutting around in soutanes, praising the Lord.' He shook his head and forced a contemptuous laugh. 'And your own situation. You're in the middle of something that you've worked hard on, and within a few days you're expected to dance to a different tune.'

He was lapsing into one of those pits of gloom he had suffered from during his final year at Maynooth, when he had taken to his bed each afternoon. Togged out and with football boots in hand, others in the corridor failed to rouse him from a Harold Robbins novel or from his rigid position at the table playing a game of patience.

That evening, Brian found himself in silent agreement with the other man's fault-finding, though he wouldn't go as far as his gloomy prediction that 'we are witnessing the death of the Church, and not before its time'.

Later, in Neary's, the mood softened; Paul talked about his work in the hospital and Brian gave an account of Melrose.

'What's this guy Leo like anyway?' Paul drained his glass and nodded to the barman.

'A big change from poor old Tim Sheridan, that's for sure. "Please" and "thanks" aren't in Leo's vocabulary.'

'How does Dick Hegarty take it?'

'Dick has opted for survival.' But Brian wanted a break from talk of Melrose. 'And you? You seem to have an awful lot of meetings in the hospital lately.'

Paul inhaled on his cigar. 'The place gets you down. A big number of deaths this winter – that's hard to take; you feel helpless and almost in the way of the doctors. I know I don't have your problem of arguing with school cleaners about wages and making out tax forms.' A smile flitted across his lips. 'I've been keeping late hours, and that doesn't help. The other night the staff had a bit of a do for one of the nurses who is getting married, and, of course, Orla and – you remember her friend? Mary Donovan. They forced me to go with them.'

Of late, Orla Clancy's name had skirted along the edges of Paul's speech. The previous summer she had written him a long letter from Greece, and the Sunday after her return, he had taken her and Mary Donovan for a drive. They had called to Beechmount on their way home.

When Brian returned to his house after officiating at baptisms that Sunday, he had glanced out of the window while filling the kettle. The three of them were lying on the grassy bank. In sunglasses and a white dress that emphasized her copper skin, Orla sat in the middle. She was resting on one elbow talking to Paul, on his back beside her. As soon as Brian opened the back door, she had held up a bunch of car keys: 'Not bad for my third lesson, Brian,' she said. 'I drove in here and around that corner.'

'And left half my tyres on the side of the kerb.' Paul pointed out an old tyre mark. She made to give him a swipe, but he shielded himself with his arms.

Wind and rain prevented the two priests from playing golf the following Thursday, so they went to a film at the Savoy and then had a drink in the Royal Dublin hotel. More than ever, Paul brought Orla's name into the conversation. At length Brian ventured to remark: 'You must be seeing each other a lot lately.'

'What are you implying, O'Neill?' Paul asked, a look of playful scepticism on his face.

'Wouldn't you need to be careful?'

'Ah, would you get on.' He explained that Orla used him as a sounding board for problems she was trying to resolve. 'Recently, one of the interns has been pestering her to go out with him.' He began to arrange the beer mats in different formations. 'No, it's nothing like that. It's just, you know yourself, some women feel safer with priests.' He paused. 'You know, O'Neill, your maturity frightens me.'

'How do you mean?'

'Well, for a start, you could loosen up a bit, relax your guard now and again.' And then because he had slipped into a vein of gravity, he drained his glass and added: 'You're worse than my mother.'

They had one more drink and returned to the presbytery.

Four

During his first weeks in Melrose, Brian was without a map in a strange country. Initially he considered starting the Parish Renewal programme, but that idea he discarded. The Vatican Council's notion of lay involvement was unlikely to arouse much interest in Melrose, where the chief concern was to stretch the social welfare allowance until the end of the week.

A succession of callers, mostly women, arrived on his doorstep; their separate stories followed a pattern. First came a litany of mishaps: they had lost a purse on the bus, or their handbag had been stolen on Moore Street, or the Vincent de Paul men hadn't called on the Thursday night and now they had no milk or bread in the house '... for the kiddies goin' to school in the morning'. He gave one woman thirty pounds to go to Limerick. She told him her son was in prison down there: 'Got mixed up with a bad crowd, Father.'

Father Hegarty laughed when he heard the story. 'Crissie has been pedalling that for a good while now. Don't be taken in by them. They always make up someone new. It was the same when Liam arrived.'

What worried Brian more than all that was his own lack of interest, as if his enthusiasm had drained away. Yet he limped along, said Mass, sat in the confessional of the empty church on a Saturday night, gave the school cleaners their cheques and notified the police when the alarm went off in Holy Trinity. After each break-in, he cleaned up the broken glass with Andy the caretaker and washed the marauders' excrement from the blue and grey tiles.

He had a chance meeting in the Veritas Bookshop with Father Luke, the spiritual director in All Saints. 'Oh, don't worry about that,' the elder assured him. 'You'll settle in; leave it in the Lord's hands. It's always the same story when a priest goes to a new parish,' he intoned in the same sing-song way he had delivered his Tuesday night talks in the oratory, when half the students were nodding off or drooping over the armrest. Did Brian play golf, he wanted to know, and did he keep up contact with his brother-priests? 'Exercise and the company of one's confrères,' Father Luke advised with a farewell touch on the arm.

That night Brian phoned Tim Sheridan.

'You didn't happen to see my white stole anywhere, Tim?'

'No, but I'll look. You may have left it in the sacristy.'

Brian thought his gambit would deflect from the real reason for phoning. He was mistaken. Tim Sheridan grew vigilant: the Brian he knew was well-organized; unlike other curates, he rarely left an alb or a breviary lying about on tables or window ledges. And when he began to complain about priests 'living on the golf courses', Sheridan decided it was time to pay a visit to Melrose. Once, he had a curate who began to find fault with everything, especially the weather: winter was wet and miserable; the few days of summer sunshine were suffocating. He was too late to pick up the signals, and the curate left for Manchester with a teacher from the comprehensive school.

The following day Brian returned from visiting the Confirmation class to find he had locked himself out: the second time in a week. He had just replaced the moulding around a new pane of glass when Tim Sheridan pulled up in front of his house.

'I was calling to see someone in the hospital, so I decided, since I'm in the area, I may as well pay you a visit.' He took stock of his surroundings. 'The new church you told me about?'

'I'll give you a tour later. Come on in.' Brian wiped the putty off his fingers and shook the parish priest's hand. 'You're most welcome.'

Over a cup of coffee, they relaxed into the flow of anecdotes that passed between them; yet beneath the chuckles, Tim Sheridan detected a strain in his friend's face. Knocking out his pipe in the ashtray, he referred, in a throwaway manner, to the class conference of a few evenings before: 'And like you said about the golf – a fair amount of gossip. There was a time when it used irritate me, but it's the same everywhere – doctors or teachers or police – when they get together.'

'You get tired of the stupid jokes.' Brian looked out the back window at the shirts he had washed that morning billowing in the wind.

'But remember, they're often a way of coping with a damn difficult sacrifice. Aren't we living in a way that was meant only for monks? And we're not in lone presbyteries like them.' He raised himself from the armchair and examined the bowl of the pipe. 'Who nowadays would give up what is probably the most powerful urge of all? And on top of that we rely on the charity of the people for maintenance. Maybe there's a lot we don't give ourselves credit for.'

'You could be right.'

They left the ponderous mood behind them in the sitting room. At the front door, Sheridan buttoned up his gaberdine overcoat. 'Yourself and Paul must come over for dinner some day.'

'I'll look forward to that.'

Father Brannigan needed help in the parish office. He was launching a new family-offering campaign, so every morning after Mass, Brian, despite the inner groan, affixed labels to envelopes and placed them in boxes for delivery. Sister Fidelis, a frail nun who worked at the other table, had taught classics for forty years and, when she retired to the Mother House, had asked to work in Melrose. She had envisaged visiting the homes of the First Communicants at her own pace, but had to remain in the office when the secretary got married and went to live in Navan.

One morning as Brian was passing through the sacristy, he overheard a woman in tears of anger upbraid Father Brannigan; he had forgotten to call out her mother's name at the anniversary Mass.

'It slipped my mind,' he pleaded.

'It didn't slip your mind to stick out your hand for the money though.'

Red-faced, the parish priest stormed into the office and after a curt 'Good morning' pulled out the steel drawers of a filing cabinet. 'Where's the Easter dues list I left here only yesterday?' he asked without turning to look at Sister Fidelis.

The nun rose from the typewriter and handed him the list; it was on the table before him. He grunted and swept past her to the photocopier. There he shuffled a ream of paper, awkwardly stuffed it into the machine and pressed the switch; the green light flowed across the plate and the typed copies dropped on the tray. He stood over the machine and had begun to hum when the smooth rhythm became a chug: a sheet in concertina folds struggled out on top of the others and the motor ground to a halt. He tried to free the paper, but it tore away in his hand. 'What did you do to the machine, Fidelis?' Anger seeped through the controlled tone.

'I haven't been using the photocopier, Father.' Her voice remained calm. 'In fact, you will recall that you yourself used it yesterday evening to run off a circular letter.'

Again he tugged at the rumpled paper, muttering and sighing as his stout fingers fumbled to no avail. Eventually he pulled over the plastic cover and sat down.

'Have you that letter ready for me?' he asked, tapping an urgent rhythm with his fingers: horses galloped on the table. The nun stopped typing, got to her feet and handed him the shivering leaf. She returned to her desk, but, instead of resuming her work, rested her forehead in the palm of her hand as if to ease a headache.

At his job of sorting the envelopes, Brian followed her every movement: her shoulders trembled and then became rigid before she got up from her chair and hurried from the office. Blind to what was happening, Brannigan half-turned towards his curate.

'Some of these Sisters,' he said, his anger now subsiding; 'they want to work in parishes and, when they are given work, they can't do it properly.'

Sister Fidelis returned after Father Brannigan had left the office; she was pale, though her eyes were red.

'I don't wish to be uncharitable,' she said, 'but that man doesn't seem to know when he is giving offence. What you saw just now was mild in comparison.'

It was the opening he was waiting for: 'Why do you give in to him, Sister?'

She removed her glasses and took a handkerchief from her sleeve. 'The options are limited for someone like me. Either I remain on here or else I join those who shuffle around corridors; in a big old convent that can be a cheerless prospect.' She replaced her glasses. 'The few we have left who are teaching have meetings every night, so there are a lot of empty spaces now.'

The ugly scene strayed into Brian's head the following night in the confessional. He stared at the red bars of the heater beside his feet and saw again the Sister's quivering shoulders and her brave effort at composure before she rushed from the office. The accusation of incompetence hurled at one who had distinguished herself with a double first at university grated all the more since it had come from a bungler. And he cursed his own lack of courage for not confronting Brannigan. Rising anger now fuelled every random thought: why did he have to remain in this blasted confinement for another hour when, like other nights, he might have only one or two stragglers? In the previous half-hour two had come: little boys who sniggered outside the confessional. 'What sins do I tell him?' A whispered instruction followed and then a boy of eight or nine sat before him in the counselling room. Wide-eyed, he took everything in: the electric fire, the purple stole around the priest's neck and the movement of the hand raised in a blessing.

'I spoiled love when I didn't share me marbles with me brother, Father.' After every few words he snuffled and wiped his nose with his sleeve.

The priest spoke the words of absolution in a half-whisper. When he had finished, the boy made a few attempts at the Act of Contrition until Brian came to his rescue. The second boy, slightly bigger, had a duplicate list. As soon as he left, there were titters of laughter until they both scurried out of the church, no longer bothering to stifle their giggles when they let the door slam.

He picked up his breviary and strolled up and down the side aisle. In the dim light, the gilt edges flashed when he flicked over a page. He passed the other curate's confessional: a purple stole hung over the open half-door.

Father Hegarty had remained hearing confessions for a few minutes after the evening Mass and, knowing that the parish priest was at a wedding reception, made his escape at the first opportunity. He had learned to fawn in the seminary and was so successful that they had made him a prefect in his final year. When he had lived in Swords, across from the Canon, he used to steal down the back garden with his golf clubs to the Station Road and wait for one of his classmates to pick him up. The Canon, who treated the curates like schoolboys, was none the wiser seeing his assistant's car in the driveway.

An old man pushed open the door of the church and made his way towards the confessional; he touched the armrests as he trundled along. As soon as he heard the sound of wheezing, Brian closed his breviary and hurried back to his post.

'Are you there, Father?' the voice called through the grill. Brian raised his hand and whispered a blessing.

'I forgot to say my prayers four mornings. Father, I told lies a few times and I missed Mass once, Father.' Then a pause to recover his breath. 'And I did bad things in my youth, Father.' Another wheezing pause. 'Women. You know.' The sediment of guilt, which had consolidated over many years, had forced the old man to return. He probably tells this every month, Brian reflected, while he raised his hand in absolution. About half-way through the prayer, the man interrupted him: 'And, Father, I did impure actions with myself. That's all, Father.'

Brian debated with himself whether he would comment or not. When he had finished, he inclined his head to the grill: 'Those sins are not as serious as you may think.'

'I'm a bit deaf, Father.'

'The sins of your youth have been absolved long ago.'

'What did you say my penance was?'

'One Our Father.'

'Thank you, Father.'

When the shuffling faded, the priest stared at the blank wall. What was he doing here on a Saturday night, he asked himself, except continuing a system that compelled an old man to come out and confess what had been nothing more than a healthy impulse? And why was it that so much of what he took for granted was now an irritant; had he lived out his priesthood with the blinkered vision of a workhorse? In the early years of his ministry, when young wives agonized over the use of contraceptives, he, a twenty-five-year-old with set answers to every problem, had no misgivings about emphasizing the importance of the Pope's encyclical on birth control. Now, as he closed the confessional and knelt to pray, he winced at the memory. Outside, a door slammed and a motor started up. When the car had faded out of earshot, the dim silence of the empty church closed in on him.

Like someone drifting off to sleep who jumps to save himself from an imaginary fall, he was startled by the crash of coins in the shrine box. Over to his left, the ghostly figure of Miss Mary Ann Cummiskey was silhouetted on the wall above the bank of vigil lights. He got to his feet and hurried to the sacristy door, rattling the keys as he went. Tonight he had no intention of listening to an account of her apparitions, nor to the catastrophes that the Blessed Virgin was predicting if the world did not turn away from its sins. From behind the sacristy door he watched her bless herself, kiss the Blessed Virgin's feet several times, and then, handbag clutched beneath her arm, stride out of the church. He gave her plenty of time to be gone before he switched off the lights in the porch and locked the main door.

'She has asked us to pray for purity, especially for priests and nuns, Father.' Out of the darkness the frantic woman had crept up from behind. 'She comes down to earth every evening at twenty to six, Father.'

'At twenty to six, Mary Ann,' he repeated and edged down the path away from her. 'I'll remember that. I have to go now and prepare the few words for the morning.'

'Pray for purity, Father.'

'I will. I'll pray for purity.'

'Will you come with us on the bus next Sunday? She appears every Sunday in Bessborough.'

'I think I'm on baptisms next Sunday, Mary Ann.' He kept on walking.

Holding fast to her handbag, she threw him a defeated 'God bless' and disappeared into the night.

To clear his head, he walked up Melrose Road past The Spanish Lady as far as the health clinic. A ghetto blaster blared in a doorway of Holy Trinity, cigarettes glowed and faded; a girl darted from the huddle and screamed for help. 'Fuck off, Ado,' she roared when chased along the front of the school. The others shouted and laughed, urging on Ado, who caught up with his prey in another doorway.

'Leave me alone, Ado,' she protested, but the cry was more an inducement than a reprimand and became a giggle as the two bodies became one bulky figure. 'Not here, Ado, not here.' Her voice was soft now as they disappeared around the corner.

To avoid the images that began to flare up in his mind, the priest hastened across the road towards his house – the only one in darkness. Another wild roar went up from the direction of the school. He could expect the principal's phone call again on Monday morning: would he notify Church & General Insurance that the Davis Towers lot had done more damage, and would he mind taking Andy to Chadwicks for the window fittings?

A couple passed by, linked and in step, the same couple he met every Saturday night on their way to the pub.

'That's a hardy one, Father,' the man said, hands secure in the pockets of his overcoat. They crossed over and continued on their journey.

Back home, Brian stoked up the dying embers, shovelled on more coal and poured himself a whiskey, leaving the bottle on the open leaf of the drinks cabinet. He sat for a while and watched the flames struggle through the shiny black lumps. He would usually be at Walshe's around this time on a Saturday night: Aidan stretched out on the studded couch, after a week of listening to his patients' description of their aches and pains; and Irene, legs curled beneath her on the other armchair, taking an occasional sip from her glass. Their scraps of conversation would mingle with their interest in the TV talk show that flickered in the corner. He could get in the car and drive across the city, as he had done in the first couple of weeks; they were delighted to see him. But he held back. His description of Melrose had met with mild amusement or else a polite veil of interest that sometimes failed to mask their indifference.

The phone interrupted his reflections. His mother was anxious to know how he was settling in.

'Fine. I'm fine.' It was an effort to be casual. 'They all tell me it takes about six months to get used to a new parish.'

'In no time at all you'll make friends.' She returned to his change of appointment before hanging up. 'As soon as Maura gets a chance, we'll go to Dublin for a few days; Kieran is very busy at present, farmers calling on him at all hours.'

While she spoke, he formed an image of the veterinary surgeon, his brother-in-law, delivering calves or injecting sick cattle and then throwing the wooden case and the green Wellingtons into the back of the Opel Estate and speeding off to the next farmyard. 'It's better to wait until the weather softens anyway.'

He stared at the television screen. Behind the assurances, she was worried and he regretted his outburst of the previous Sunday night, but she had caught him at a bad moment; he had opened fire on '… bishops who treat priests like messenger boys'. Her outward confidence was typical of a woman who had stood up to cattle-dealers until his brother, Donal, was old enough to take over.

'A woman will never be able for that farm,' the neighbours had predicted when his father had passed away. Delia O'Neill, however, showed the same strength that had taken her, one of eight children, from a labourer's cottage to ward sister in a London hospital until a vacancy had arisen in St Camillus's and she could return to Ireland. For sure, she would take a dim view of this lazing around. He gave the whiskey glass a twirl before taking a mouthful and reaching for the remote control.

Five

In Beechmount, he had visited the school nearly every morning, had coffee with the teachers at ten-thirty and, in summertime, helped to transport children to Ashgrove Lawn Tennis Club. Now whenever he passed by Holy Trinity, the grey building became a reproach to his negligence. Frequent phone calls from the principal, Muredach Hogan, to order oil or call a meeting of the school committee, would force him to discharge his managerial duties. And he knew that if he didn't visit the classrooms before long, the principal would, in his sly way, whisper it to the parish priest.

'Be careful with Muredach; he runs with every story to Leo,' Dick Hegarty had cautioned him. 'They used to fish Lough Sheelin together and then Leo appointed him after he left the Brothers.'

One morning when fog had almost hidden Davis Towers, Brian trudged across the yard to the main door. He nodded to a couple of women smoking cigarettes outside the principal's office. One had a grip on the handlebar of a go-cart; inside the plastic cover a child looked out at him and smiled.

Avoiding the infants' section, he continued along the corridor, away from the sing-song chorus, until he reached the senior classes: he would be able to make some contact with them.

He was about to knock when he heard a woman's voice:

'Remember, children, out of love comes poetry, music and song, and so when we try it again, think of the poet composing for his loved one. I'll play it once more and then we'll sing it all together. Listen.'

While she played the piano, he stood rooted to the spot. A couple of children with copybooks hurried by and he pretended to be examining the ceiling as if for a leak.

Like peering through a misted window pane, he caught the outline of a boyhood memory: his mother playing the same tune and he looking out at the forsythia bushes in their gilded glory.

'*Fáilte romhat, a athair.*' The children reeled off the greeting while he searched the faces until he saw the teacher rise from the piano.

'*Go raibh maith agaibh a leanai agus a mhuinteoir.* Don't let me disturb you.' He introduced himself and shook the teacher's hand.

'Niamh Kirwan. You're welcome to the parish.' She motioned for the class to sit. They were preparing for a choral festival, she said.

'Would it be too much to ask if I could hear that song again?' He turned to the crop of faces.

The soft upturn at the corners of her mouth gave her a remarkably girlish look. 'Come on now and don't let me down before our visitor.'

She pointed to the lyrics on the blackboard and tripped to the piano stool, a restless energy in her movements. While they sang, he followed the words in copperplate writing:

> '*Tis the last rose of summer*
> *Left blooming alone*
> *All her lovely companions*
> *Are faded and gone;*
> *No flower of her kindred,*
> *No rosebud is nigh.*
> *To reflect back her blushes,*
> *or give sigh for sigh.*

He lingered on the downward tilt of her head and the sheen where her dark hair caught the light. His gaze settled on the hands that coaxed a melody from the keys. Instinctively, he took in the shapely figure in the tartan skirt and the white blouse, but as soon as he awakened to the thoughts that had slipped his guard, he returned to the blackboard.

'We're visiting the Botanic Gardens some day, Father,' she said when they had finished. 'We're going to see the rose tree that was taken from the garden where Thomas Moore wrote that song.'

While they were chatting, a girl approached them. 'Mrs Kirwan, look.' She held up a flashy-looking biro. 'Me brother bought me a gold pen in Liverpool. He was over for a match.'

'Yes. That's lovely.'

When the child had returned to her seat, Mrs Kirwan lowered her voice: 'That's the nearest you'll ever get, child, to a gold pen.'

She asked them to read over the lyrics.

'Big change, I imagine, from your last parish.'

He gave a little laugh. 'You've no idea.' The inclination was to reveal the storm he had run into since the archbishop's letter, but he skirted along the margin, recounting, with a semblance of good humour, the commonplace chores he would have to get used to until he found a housekeeper.

'Can you cook at least?' She had a look of amusement on her face.

'Enough to keep away starvation.'

But she wasn't listening. Her look had changed: she was a cat ready to pounce. He followed her gaze to the back of the room where two children were whispering and sniggering, the only ones unaware of the teacher's displeasure. The creeping silence caused them to raise their heads; and, for what seemed a very long time, they were left to squirm beneath the stare.

'I'll deal with you later' was enough to command every head to sink.

She turned to him, her anger replaced with a playful grin. 'You have to let them see who is boss,' she whispered, and then began to search her desk, lifting copies and a lunch box until she found two tickets. 'There,' she said. 'The choral festival is on in June, in the National Concert Hall. A welcome-to-Melrose for you.'

From bringing communion to a few sick people and delivering family-offering boxes to collectors, he had acquired a working knowledge of the parish; however, to fill out the picture, he decided to take a walk. One afternoon, he set his face against the March wind that swept down Melrose Road from the tower block. Ahead of him shirts and sheets billowed over the balconies of the high-rise flats. Two floors up a woman in a wrap-around overall beat dust out of a mat. Below her, children kicked a ball, and a spray of mud showered the clothes line. She whipped the cigarette out of her mouth: 'Get the fuck out of there. Do youse see what youse have done to me washin'?' The boys abandoned the football and scurried around the corner.

'Them is bold boys, Father.' A little girl eyed the priest from behind the palisade fencing that surrounded Davis Towers; others left the swings and thrust their faces through gaps where the slats were missing or bent. Like birds on a telegraph wire, a row of heads jutted through the metal strips.

'He comes into our class. Don't youse come to our class, Father? Tells us all about Holy God so he does.' This was followed by a chorus: 'Hello Father O'Neill.' He waved and continued on his way.

At the corner of a cul-de-sac, children were gathered at the open side of a blue van that sold groceries, sweets and cigarettes. The wheels had been removed and concrete blocks had been wedged beneath the base. Farther down on a grassy patch were the charred remains of a burned-out car.

A boy, of nine or ten, darted from the group, and the van owner, a dark-skinned little man with a handlebar moustache, gave chase.

'Run, Darren, he's behind you,' the others shouted. The man grabbed the boy, whipped a packet out of his hand and aimed a kick at his backside, but the boy escaped.

'You fuckin' monkey, you eye-talian fuckin' monkey,' the boy yelled, running in the direction of the abattoir. 'I'll tell me Da and he'll burn down your fuckin' gaff.'

Brian completed the full circle, and, approaching the church from the other end of the parish, decided to go in and say a prayer. He sat at the back and allowed his mind to range freely over the afternoon stroll. After some time, the cold crept up through him. As he stood to leave, a woman came in and knelt a couple of seats in front.

. On his way out, he stopped to examine the notices in the porch. Pinned to the board were announcements about bingo, phone numbers for the Natural Family Planning Service, and posters advertising Knock, Fatima and Medjugorje.

A draft of wind at the door made it difficult for the woman to manoeuvre her shopping trolley; he rushed to her assistance. 'Not easy on a day like this,' he said.

'That's the least of my problems. It's draggin' this over the pedestrian bridge that I dread. I wish we had a decent super-market here.'

She hoped he was settling in. 'It can't be that easy gettin' used to a place like this, but we're not too bad once you know us.'

She was on the Melrose Youth Committee; at present they were trying to get those that drank cider beneath the bridge to go on a community work programme. 'Sometimes,' she admitted, 'you feel like you're hittin' your head against a stone wall. Maybe when you're settled in, you might give us a hand. Didn't you used to be involved with youth in your last parish?'

'I'll do whatever I can.' He paused. 'We haven't met.'

'Phyllis Jordan.'

'If I can help in any way, let me know.'

'I'll take you up on that. And, by the way, if you're at a loose end, you're always welcome to drop down. We live at number sixteen, The Grove.'

Over a cup of coffee in his house, he took up Liam Holden's *Status Animarum*. When he opened the notebook containing a list of all the parishioners, an ordination leaflet slipped from between the pages. On the card was his predecessor's name in bold print, and above it, a quotation from Ignatius of Loyola: 'To give and not to count the cost, to labour and to seek for no reward, save that of knowing thy holy will.' Along the bottom, it read:

> Please pray for my father, brothers and sister and all who helped me to become a priest. Grant eternal rest to my mother's soul.

After each visit, Liam Holden had ticked the page and had

added a comment here and there: 'No Mass' or 'Refused to give to family offering. He said they were broke.' Whenever he had been left standing at the doorstep, he recorded the impoliteness in red biro. In the last page he had written: 'Visitation of Melrose and Davis Towers complete. Alleluia. 16/12/1984.'

Brian closed the notebook. He calculated the date to be about two years after Liam had come to the parish: it must have been then that he had given up and taken to birdwatching down at Bull Island.

'Poor ould Liam,' Dick had told him. 'Found Melrose too much, and Brannigan hounding him for bank statements of the school account. So he went off every day with the binoculars round his neck. I doubt if he took them off even when he went to bed.'

Brian determined that he was not going to become another Liam Holden, and the only way to conquer his lack of interest was to begin house-to-house visitations as he had done in Beechmount.

A few weeks later he braced himself for his task. There was no response to the metallic tap of the cheap knocker from the first two houses. A woman with children peeping out from behind her stood at the next door; she turned to slap a demanding child, displaying a pink slip where the zip of her skirt had burst. On her feet were a pair of worn slippers.

When the bawling child had disappeared inside, the woman launched an attack on the parish priest.

'An do you know what I'm goin' to tell you an' you're a priest. He shouldn't be in this parish. You never see him. They do say he's always in some library in Pearse Street readin' old newspapers.'

The nodding concern encouraged her to continue: 'An' another thing. I sent my Amanda an' her friend for holy water an' he ran them out of the Church of God. Now, Father? He said they were disturbin' his prayer. As true as God, I had to borra' me neighbour's Valium before I went up to him.'

There was nothing for him to do except listen and, when he got an opening, he said: 'I'm just making a brief visit to get to know the people.' He shook her moist hand and promised to call again.

A glance at Liam Holden's *Status Animarum* revealed that the neighbours, whose house he was about to enter, neither went to Mass nor subscribed to the weekly envelope. On the footpath he had to avoid a child who was swinging around in a tyre, roped to the lamp post; others gave her a push whenever she lost pace.

'Do you want a go, Father O'Neill?'

'Some other time. Thanks.'

Holding back the knocker so that it wouldn't crash down on the metal plate, he tapped and steeled himself for an answer. One of the standards supporting the canopy over the door had become loose and hung drunkenly in the air; patches of oil stained the driveway and a rusted car axle lay beneath the front window.

Inflating a chewing-gum bubble between her teeth, a girl answered the door.

'I'm Father O'Neill,' he began. 'I'm new to the parish and I'm making a brief visit to the homes.'

While he spoke, she fixed him with a blank look and continued to work on the bubble.

'Ma, you're wanted at the door,' she shouted into the hallway.

'Who?' came the reply.

'You.'

'Who wants me?'

'The priest wants you.' She turned and ambled inside. A woman waddled to the door. Strands of hair hung limply about her flushed face.

'Sorry, Father. Come in. That Mary has no manners.' She led him through to the back. The hallway was cold and reeked of sweat. In the sitting room she scolded Mary, who lay sprawled beside the fire. A small boy, naked except for a vest streaked with dribble, stood before the television; the flickering screen cast a sickly colour on his face. He eyed the priest and toddled over to him, offering a plastic mug with a mouthpiece on the lid. Drops of tea spilled on to the Brian's polished shoes.

'No thanks. That's your tea and you don't want to give away

your tea like that now.' Angered by the refusal, the child flung the mug. It hit the side of Brian's chair and rolled along the floor.

'Jason,' shouted the woman, 'stop that. Mary, take Jason out while I'm talking to the priest.'

Murmuring a protest, Mary raised herself from the chair, grabbed Jason by the shoulder and dragged him out of the room. When the screaming had faded, the woman lowered the television and shoved her chair beside the priest. 'That's Mary's young lad, Father. The chap she was going with; he's no good.' She shook her head. 'I tried to talk to her but she wouldn't listen.' She spoke to his profile as if she were in confession.

The family had left the two-room tenement in Gardiner Street where they always had someone dropping in.

'Out here, Father, you could be dead and no one would care. We should never have left. I've had no luck in this house. You're never the same after a change from one place to another, Father.'

'Sorry to hear that things haven't been working out.'

After Mary came Tony who was in St Patrick's Institution for Young Offenders. He had assaulted the van owner in Melrose Avenue with a stick and had taken the cash box. Jacqueline worked in Cadbury's and Tommy was on probation; he had been caught smoking hash under the bridge.

'You'll have to come and bless the house,' she said at the door. 'It might bring us luck.'

'I will of course.' He shook her hand.

'Bless the house, bless the house,' he raged to himself as he strode up Melrose Road. 'Sprinkle holy water. Say the magic words and all will be well again.' The tumult closed in on him: the grating of the football along the road, the shouts of children swinging around the lamp posts – their faces pale beneath the street lights seemed to grin like mischievous monkeys when they chorused his name.

A woman in a plastic overall rushed through a gate and climbed the steps of the white minibus parked at the kerb.

'I nearly missed you,' she told the driver. 'You're not usin' your ding-dong this evenin', Jimmy.' The other women joined her in a guffaw. 'Oh Jimmy uses his ding-dong alright,' one of them said. They climbed into the minibus and drove off. On the side of the minibus was a list of services provided by Noonan's Office Cleaners.

Across from The Spanish Lady, a boy stood beneath a lamp post eating a packet of crisps; above his head the light showed the slanting fall of rain. Something in the boy's hang-dog look caused Brian to slow his steps.

'Good evening,' he said.

'Howya?'

As if they spoke a different language, the reply stressed the gap between them, so that Brian was tempted to keep going. He had had enough for one day; the doleful expression, however, dragged him back. He tried again.

'Looks like it's going to be a bad night.'

The boy smiled and shrugged. After another awkward moment, he extended the packet: 'Have a crisp, Father.'

'Thanks.' To avoid giving offence he reached into the packet, ransacking his mind to find the right wavelength between them. The boy rescued him. 'You're goin' around to the houses, Father.'

'That's right.'

'Will you say a prayer for us, Father?'

'Sure. What will ... is there something special? Anyone sick?'

'Me ma is gone.'

'Gone?'

'Last week her an' me da had a row. He's been in the pub ever since. This evenin' he came home from the Melrose an' threw me out. He said: "All that comes out of your mouth is shite".' The boy kicked a stone against the school wall. 'I was tryin' to tell him about the metalwork we're doin' at the Tech.'

'I'm sorry to hear about the trouble you're going through.' He felt in his pocket: three pounds wrapped around coins as he'd got it in change earlier that day.

'There. You might be able to get something for yourself. Will I call later?'

'No, Father, no. Me da would give me a hidin' if he thought I'd told you.'

'I'll call some other day so.' He took a note of the boy's address.

He had almost passed by the car parked in front of Holy Trinity when a woman's voice reached him. 'That's a serious look you're wearing.' She inclined her head through the open window.

'Niamh, isn't it?' He concealed his eager recognition. Ever since that first day in her classroom, he had begun to spend more time in the school, and to relieve the tedium of inspecting artwork and affecting wonder while he moved between the desks, he saved the visit to her class until the end. Sometimes he played the piano and convinced himself that he was helping with the preparations for Confirmation.

'Hop in from the shower for a minute.' She leaned across and opened the passenger door. 'I'm waiting for the children; we're having a choir practice.'

An odd feeling crept over him while they were speaking in the car. They were removed from the everyday background of children's voices and the smell of chalk and blackboards, and it seemed as if he had known this woman in the trench coat all his life. With her, the rumble that had assaulted his brain ceased: the factory hooters and the growl of lorries out of the industrial estate faded.

'It must be very different from your last parish.' She switched off the windscreen wipers.

'Well,' he hesitated, watching the rain smear the view again, 'they have their problems too in Beechmount.'

'You're wary. Does that come with the job or the fact that you're from Kerry?'

'Both.'

A few children ran towards them and sheltered in the lee of the pillars. 'I'd better be going,' she said, reaching for her basket in the back seat. 'Will you come out to the house some night? Shane is in London these weeks. When he's back, we'll fix a time.'

'That would be good.'

In his house, without putting on the light, he went straight for the front room to draw the curtains, but the rain streaming down the window pane held his attention. Hands buried deep in his overcoat, he looked out at the bleak scene. After a while the forlorn face of the boy with the crisps came back to him.

A crash of broken glass away to the right caused him to raise the net curtain. Three horses thundered across the green, their riders shouting and roaring, and flinging stones at the roof of the old library. When the riders had gained the embankment and were on Melrose Road, the galloping hooves rampaged through the winter streets. He turned back to the library. Abandoned now, the granite building with its splendid pediment and corbels appeared to suffer in silence its latest indignity. Dark patches on the glistening roof showed where slates had fallen off.

He lowered the curtain, but remained fixed on the library. Slowly, like light seeping into a room from the hallway when someone edges in the door, the darkness receded from his mind. He began to make connections. He heard Phyllis Jordan saying, 'Maybe when you're settled in you might give us a hand out,' and he saw the defeated eyes of the boy with the packet of crisps.

The dream took shape: instead of the scowling block now blurred and disfigured by the trickle of raindrops, he saw a light in every window and young people no longer having to huddle beneath the railway bridge.

The youth council had given him a grant to transform an old stable in Beechmount into a youth clubhouse. The same would happen here, he knew, except that he would need a lot more money. Maybe Brannigan would make a contribution from one of the parish accounts if he asked at the right time. The vision was flowing so sweetly, he refused to allow for obstacles.

After the seven-thirty Mass he checked the answering machine: Father Sheridan wanted to know if he would come for lunch the following Thursday.

He returned his call. 'I had planned to meet Paul in the afternoon, Tim. We're heading for Glendalough – anywhere as far away as possible from here.'

'Bring him along and whenever you want to go, you can.'

'Perfect.'

The following morning in the sacristy, when he revealed his plan for the library to Dick Hegarty, his hopes of the previous night turned out to be a false dawn.

'Good idea,' the other priest agreed, 'but you'll be up against

Morgan. He has his greedy eye on that for a video shop and a take-away.'

'That's the guy that drives a Mercedes. You pointed him out at a funeral.'

'That's Terence A. Morgan. Has political aspirations, you know.'

While Dick Hegarty spoke, Brian saw his plan waste away and the gloom that had enveloped his world since arriving in Melrose returned.

On the Thursday, Father Sheridan's housekeeper opened the door for the two priests. The graze of the Venetian blind against the door and the faint smell of tobacco had the same effect on Brian as looking at old photographs. The layout of the sitting room recalled the July evening he got his first introduction to parish life after doing his chaplaincy stretch in one of the vocational schools. Nothing had changed. The model in silver of a pylon, mounted on mahogany, rested on the sideboard: a well-deserved gift from the people of Roundwood.

In the early fifties, when Sheridan had been in County Wicklow, he had cycled to every house in the parish dispelling resistance to the electricity supply scheme. A jumble of ancient fears of incurring debts, and deep-rooted connections with landlords formed in sheep farmers' minds. With the help of other priests and school teachers, his campaign had had a widespread effect. And they chose him to switch on the light in the village for the first time.

The three priests were relaxing into conversation when the housekeeper called them to their meal. Tim laid the pipe in an ashtray and placed it on the marble mantel. 'Ready when you are, Eileen,' he replied and led the way through the double doors.

The long window at the back provided a view of the harbour. This splendid prospect was what caught everyone's attention on entering the dining room, prompting confrères to compliment Tim on his good fortune: 'You fell on your feet when you were appointed here.'

Beechmount was considered a plum parish, a reward for his labours in Wicklow, but Sheridan retained the simplicity he had brought with him through forty-seven years of priesthood. Scarcely a day went by when he didn't set off in the afternoon to visit his parishioners.

The aperitif and the wine were beginning to have an effect on Brian; the hoops that had bound him for the past weeks fell away. He had intended revealing some of his discontent, but decided against it. He would enjoy the breather.

Afterwards, while Sheridan was relighting his pipe in the sitting room, he asked, as if in afterthought: 'How is Leo getting on?'

Brian knew him too well for the act to hold; Sheridan was concerned and it would be futile to pretend. The liqueur had given him courage. 'Fine – so long as Dick Hegarty and myself dance attendance. He checks to see if our cars are in at night.'

'That's a new one.' He chuckled. 'He usen't be like that. I had left All Saints by the time Leo was a student, but he worked in a neighbouring parish, and all I can say is that you couldn't find a more obliging fellow. They loved him in Roundwood. When he went there first, the old parish priest was riddled with arthritis, and every night Leo put him to bed and dressed him again in the morning. And that went on for about six or seven years until the man's death.'

'Are we talking about the same Leo?' Paul asked.

'Yeah, that's the frightening thing. Something snapped. I don't know – maybe it's this crazy life we lead.'

At the hall door he said to Brian: 'Drop over some Sunday night and we'll go for a stroll.'

The smile died as Sheridan watched them go down the granite steps and drive off.

Turning off the main road at Kilmacanogue, Paul, as if he had been carrying on a conversation with himself, said: 'Isn't it scary?'

'What?'

'Whatever happened to Leo. You know – so willing – and the way he looked after the old parish priest.' He answered his own question: 'Sheridan is right: it's a dog's life we lead.'

On the way to Glendalough, Brian noticed that his friend was lapsing into one of his silences and found himself struggling to bring a spark to the conversation; even then, the replies were dead offerings, as though his mind was elsewhere.

They parked beside the turf-brown waters and crossed to the other side of the lake by the narrow bridge; their feet sounding on the wooden planks, then quiet again on the soft covering of pine needles that sloped up the hillside. From down by the lake came the lonesome cry of a curlew.

They were half-way through their second drink in The Yellow House before Paul revealed the source of his gloom. 'I may as well tell you. You are looking at a fallen cleric.' The forced smile faded: 'I mean Orla and myself.'

On the previous Sunday night they had returned from a stroll around Bray Head. Mary Donovan, who shared the flat with Orla, was down the country on a few days' leave and, in the freedom afforded them, they had succumbed to a mutual craving. 'Right before the fire,' he reflected as if still trying to come to terms with the reality.

Brian masked his surprise in a reassuring tone: 'You're not the first and you won't be the last. Sure, it's understandable, after all. We make too much of it because of our background.' Absolutions fell easily from his lips.

'I know all that but it's not going to happen again.' He made a firm purpose of amendment to the half-empty glass.

Within a week the vow had been broken and now a pattern emerged: whenever the other nurse was away, he stayed overnight with Orla. Then came the confessions and the remorse and the fears that she might be pregnant and the counting of days until the end of the month.

Eventually, Brian confronted him. 'Why are you taking the risk? I mean nowadays, well, there are ways and means.'

'I couldn't. No. That would be too .... No, you don't shake off seven years in Maynooth that quickly.'

From then on a change came about in the relationship between the two friends. Paul seemed restless on their day off; after the game of golf he had a variety of excuses, too overdone to be genuine: emergency meetings; the matron would 'blow a fuse' if he were absent.

One Saturday evening while Brian was in the confessional

waiting until it was time to lock the church, there was a knock on the door and someone in a pronounced city accent called to him:

'Father, will youse hear me confession?'

He was about to replace the purple stole he'd taken off while reading the newspaper, when Paul thrust his head through the velvet curtain. 'Relax, Father,' he grinned. 'Are you nearly finished?'

'Did you see anyone out there?'

'No one, except,' and silently he formed the words with his lips, 'an oul' one kissing a statue.'

Brian had to repeat the act of rattling his keys before Miss Cummiskey blessed herself and touched the feet of the Blessed Virgin; then, storming past the two priests, she muttered something about being hunted from the house of God, and how disgraceful it was, especially by a priest.

'Who is she?' Paul asked.

'Mary Ann Cummiskey. A poor unfortunate who is on her own since her brother died.'

The breezy manner that Brian sensed in the other man on the way to the Marine Hotel was in accord with the sun-tanned figure that sat opposite him in the lounge. The face, which of late had taken on a gloomy look, now radiated health, and the loose-limbed posture suggested one who was celebrating a newfound peace. When the lounge girl had left them with their two drinks, Paul leaned forward and rested his elbows on the table. 'Look, I may as well be straight. I feel I owe you the truth about Easter. I'm sorry I couldn't join you in Kerry.'

'The first time in seven years.'

They sometimes stayed in the Dingle hostel, reserved every Easter for priests and students from All Saints and Maynooth. Overlooking the rugged coastline of Dunquin, where spray lashed and spent itself against the rocks on Clogher Strand, the extended bungalow provided a morning vista on the possibilities of the day ahead: would they race to Cumeenoole or pack sandwiches and venture up Mount Brandon?

Brian looked intent in removing the cellophane from a cigar, but he was waiting for his friend's explanation.

'There are a few things I want to come clean about. I spent a few days in Connemara with Orla. I'm in love with her, and she with me.' He hesitated and then spoke the words his friend feared. 'I'm packing the whole thing in.'

'Before you do that,' Brian looked at him, 'would you not … I mean, consider going to one of those retreat houses in England? To think it out.'

'No. I'm finished with retreats and spiritual direction.'

'And you're certain it's not, well, infatuation?'

'This is not an adolescent crush. This is probably the first adult decision I've made in my life. I've thought about this for a long time. All my life I've had someone deciding my future.' He spoke like one now free of a burden. 'In my final year in Maynooth, in fact, the February before I took Diaconate, I asked for another year to think about it. They sent me to Lenehan who was then back from Rome.'

'Yes, he gave us a Day of Recollection one time.'

'He may have been a great academic and theologian, but he knew damn all about human nature. Do you know what he said? "Everyone experiences panic coming up to ordination. You'll make a fine priest, Paul. My advice is go ahead and be ordained." How could I have been so blind?'

He was angry at the way he had been steered into the seminary. Angry at a mother who had sent him on an annual fishing holiday with her brother, the Monsignor, a vicar general in California. 'I was the one that was fucking hooked.' His regret dissolved in laughter at his own quip. After serving the uncle's Mass, he would breakfast with him at the hotel overlooking the Corrib. 'There was no chance – none whatever – to consider another way of life. She had her plan: Barry to take over from Dad, Niall to do Law and yours truly for the Church.' He relit his cigar. 'And then of course being quarantined from girls, as if they had a government health warning.'

'Do they know at home yet?'

'No, and that's what I'm dreading. You know how hysterical she can be.'

Brian knew. He had seen both sides of Clare Duggan: the charm in the eyes which in a flash could radiate poison, like the evening the maid was wheeling out the trolley and tea had spilled on the rug. Whenever he had stayed in the house, he'd seen the way she checked if they had said their Office.

And he remembered the cententary Mass in the hospital, when nurses were swishing around in their uniforms and blue capes, and telling her how great Father Paul was to the patients. Amidst the party talk and laughter in the parlour, a student joked, 'And all the nurses are mad about him, Mrs Duggan.'

Like the drop of a guillotine, the gold-toothed smile vanished and burning coals were trained on the innocent face: 'If anyone dares to lead my son from his sacred calling, woe betide her. She'll have me to deal with.'

Six

The worst time for Brian was the few moments after waking, when so many doubts attacked with added force, as if what he suppressed during the day was now taking revenge while his guard was sluggish. The questions, the dull pain, the feeling that he was drifting from what had anchored his life until then – all these grew more frightening with Paul's revelation. Yet he refused to examine the cloud that hung over his days; instead, he set his face for Melrose every afternoon. He was making progress. Soon he would be finished with that estate; then he would tackle Davis Towers.

When the parishioners realized he wasn't the bearer of bad news or looking for money, cups of tea, despite his protests, were placed at his side. 'You're the first priest we saw since we came out here. The priests were always in the houses when we were in Killarney Street' became an indirect acknowledgment of his visit. He knew from Liam Holden's notebook that the remark was untrue, but accepted the morsel of reward. It compensated in part for the hooded looks from men who continued to watch the three o'clock from Haydock Park, or else rustled the *Daily Mirror* while shame-faced wives struggled to keep the conversation going.

He tried to find common ground: the Cup Final in May; the local soccer team; Dublin's chances for the All-Ireland. The attempts failed. And one evening, to show that such sweeteners were in vain, he received a dart from a man who had read in *The Sun* that the world had come out of a big explosion: 'There's human bein's on the other planets: Mars and Jupiter. So the Garden of Eden is only a child's story.'

That Thursday he had lunch on his own in the Royal Dublin Hotel and mooched around later in the Veritas Bookshop, where he stumbled upon a video and booklets for Confirmation classes – exactly what Niamh was looking for.

'That's for you,' he said to her the next day. 'I mean, for your class.'

She removed the brown paper wrapping. 'Children,' she said, holding up the video, 'see what Father O'Neill has brought us. What do you say?'

'Thank you, Father O'Neill.'

'I'll get Muredach to reimburse you,' she whispered.

He raised both hands. 'I wouldn't hear of it.'

He was about to leave when she said: 'Isn't there an invitation long overdue? Shane is home this week, so how about Friday night?'

'Perfect.'

She wrote down her name and address on a memory slip and gave him directions. 'You'll find it easily enough. Just beyond Donabate. When you come to the Old Forge Pub, it's the first on the right.'

Ground lights illuminated the perished daffodils as he drove up the avenue leading to 'The Willows'. A Doberman pinscher started barking and trying to leap over a wire netting.

He took a bottle of wine from the back seat, and, when he emerged from the car, light from above the Georgian door caused him to turn round. Niamh was coming towards him. 'That dog is a menace.'

'Necessary, I suppose.'

'Shane thinks so. Anyway, welcome to The Willows.'

As they went in, he spotted, through one of the front windows, a bald-headed man bent over a computer.

She placed the bottle of wine on a pier table and knocked on a door leading off the hallway. 'I'll get himself.'

A shirty 'Yes' came from inside. She half-opened the door and said: 'Father O'Neill is here, Shane.'

'I'll be out in a minute.'

'Work, always work.' She led him down a couple of steps and along a narrow passage, her high heels making clean taps on the chequered floor. 'The Doss, we call this.' She opened the door into a low-ceilinged room; in a cast-iron fireplace, a bank of coal glowed below the dim light from the wall lamps.

'There's only Shane and myself. The two girls are at some debate or other in Trinity. Sonya is doing her B. Comm. this year, and Andrea is in First Arts. There they are.' She pointed to a picture on the mantelpiece. 'Sonya's Confirmation. They've grown a lot since.'

She opened a brass inlaid cabinet. 'What would you like to drink?'

'A whiskey would be fine.'

She poured a sherry for herself.

'Now,' she said, 'I'll have to be rude and check the cooking department. Rest yourself.' She indicated one of the leather armchairs, and, before leaving, inserted a tape into the sound system. He recognized Vivaldi's *Four Seasons* as her high heels receded down the passage. After a while he heard a murmur of voices: the mood was hostile. A door banged. He returned to Vivaldi, but was interrupted by approaching footsteps.

Behind her stood the bald man he had noticed at the computer.

'Father O'Neill.' He almost clicked his heels. 'Shane Kirwan.' He refilled Brian's glass and poured a gin and tonic for himself.

During the meal, Shane gave them both a lecture on sailing and on the merits of his yacht. He invited Brian to crew for him that summer. 'I could do with a big strong fellow like you.' Opening a second bottle of wine, he sniffed the cork, and spelled out what to look for when buying a good wine.

The meal over, they returned to the sitting room; Shane slumped into the couch and sipped his wine. Now, however, his 'correct' accent began to slip, and was replaced by a midlands drawl. When Niamh brought the conversation round to Melrose and Brian's youth centre, her husband jeered. 'Youth centre. I know the youth centre I'd give them. Bloody buggers tried to take my BMW. Imagine. Out this distance. If they got the two barrels up the hole that I fired that night, they wouldn't come back for a while.' He stretched out his legs, belched and dozed off.

To deflect from her husband's incivility, Niamh heightened her interest in Brian's back-to-work scheme and when Kirwan began to snore, she joked: "Now isn't that in itself grounds for divorce?' She made excuses. He had been working long hours lately: his accountancy firm had recently opened branches in Arklow and Navan. 'And the way business is today.'

'Oh I understand perfectly, Niamh.'

For her sake, he waited until a favourable moment when he made a show of surprise at discovering the time. He dissuaded her from waking her husband. 'I know well, Niamh, how tired a man can be.'

They lingered in the hallway until he heard a toilet being flushed in the back of the house.

That night he dreamt he had been locked into a church in Rome. He was suffocating and ran to every door, but all were bolted. He had to get away or he would smother. Somehow he managed to escape down a long chequered hallway leading to his parents' room. His mother sat there alone. As she held him, he could feel the consoling heat of her body, but when she raised a glass of water to his lips, he realized she was wearing Niamh Kirwan's dress.

Every month the priests met in the parochial house, a meeting known throughout the diocese as The Divide. According to custom, they added up the income from the Sunday collections, stipends from baptisms, marriages and funerals; these were entered into a ledger and divided pro rata among them.

At the May meeting, the remainder of the Easter dues had swelled each priest's income, so Father Brannigan was humming while he tied the mouths of the coin sacks and handed the ledger for signing to his two curates.

The time was right, Brian estimated, for making his proposal. He had done his homework. One afternoon, in a glass-partitioned office, a civil servant had explained that the Corporation had no plans for the library and would be prepared to lease it out to the parish for a nominal rent. 'Of course,' he added, 'considering the state it is in, you'd need an ocean of money to do what you have in mind.' He gazed at the priest for a moment: they could hear the taps of the typewriters coming from other cubicles. The official leaned across the desk: 'If you move quickly, you could be in for a government subsidy.' He wrote on a slip of paper. 'He's your man if you want a grant.'

'The Department of Labour told me they would give nine-tenths of the grant to do it up.' Brian looked at Brannigan and then at Hegarty.

The purr that had earlier rippled from the parish priest now ceased; caution tipping towards a scowl showed on his face. 'You know that isn't our job – setting up amenities like that. That's for the social workers. If we take this now, we'll be stuck with it and it'll be our responsibility. What about your successor? You're not going to be here for ever. Maybe he wouldn't like to be lumbered with a youth centre. And what else did you say would go on there?'

'A place where people could be trained to go back to work. It must be soul-destroying for those men who have nothing to do all day.'

Thinking that he should row in with the mood of the parish priest, Dick Hegarty said: 'Don't be fooled by their complaints. They would run a mile if you offered them work; sure, that's what they saw growing up, in there around Sherriff Street.'

Brian changed tack. 'If we don't act quickly, I have it from a few different sources that Morgan is after it for a video shop and a take-away. Isn't that so?' He turned to Dick, but got no support.

The idea appalled Brannigan. He despised Morgan, whom he saw as a Johnny-come-lately: a bouncer who now owned a couple of nightclubs in the city. Unconsciously he began to smooth a bushy eyebrow. Despite his reluctance to foot the bill for what he considered to be a risky venture, admiration for the young priest's dream crept up on him, and, like someone hearing the undertone of far off music that connects with what is now lost, he glimpsed traces of his own zeal. But he nipped the budding sympathy: 'You'll be responsible to the archbishop's house if this flops.'

'It won't.' Brian insisted.

'No, Leo. I'd say when Brian gets the bit between his teeth, he'll make a go of it.'

'We'll see.'

After the meeting, the two curates returned to Greenoaks Lawn. Dick pulled up at his garage door and before he took the key from the ignition, said, 'Fair play to you. You stood up well to Leo. He can be a right arsehole at times. His vintage are all the same.' A watchful eye checked the driving mirror. 'You have to play ball with him, but you're right not to take any shit. That's what happened to poor oul' Liam.' Dick himself never let Leo bully him. 'When I came here, he tried it on. I said: "Look here Leo, I'm ordained just the same as you and I'm not taking that from you." That shut him up.'

Though still smarting from the grudging attitude of the parish priest, Brian had to contain his amusement at the speech. As he listened, he remembered the eye-service games Dick played with Brannigan, but he nodded and made sounds of agreement.

In Royal Dublin Golf Club that Thursday, Looby had another sex joke when they withdrew to the corner of the lounge. Then he had a poser: 'How do you bring light to a woman's eyes?'

'Tell us, Looby. We can't wait.' Paul said, a wintry grin on his face.

'You shine a torch in her ear.'

His high-pitched laugh caused the barman to glance over and smile. Lynsky had news about the Diocesan Commission for Marriage and the Family. One of the auxiliary bishops had asked him to get it under way.

'That is for your own ears, of course; it won't be official until the autumn,' he told them, in a manner that conveyed a special standing with the bishops.

'What can you do when you are summoned by the chief?' Lynsky said.

'Ours is not to reason why.' Brian winked across at Paul.

'More or less,' Lynsky answered, so self-absorbed he was blind to the taunt.

Brian found himself grow weary of the all-too familiar pattern of their meetings: with minor variations, the days seemed to fuse together in endless boredom. He drifted in and out of the conversation; heard again Looby's plan for the parish pilgrimage to Lourdes and the number of people he had brought back to the sacraments through house visitations.

He was anxious to know about Paul's situation and as soon as they had parted from the others, he suggested, on their way into town, that they take a stroll on Dollymount Strand.

'I finally broke the news,' Paul told him after they had parked at the turn-off from the Howth Road. Sea smells rose from the mud banks at both sides. 'It was much worse than I expected. I drove down to the house last Friday night when I knew Dad would be home early. Orla waited for me in The Grand. We watched television for a while – some stupid comedy. You can imagine how I felt seeing them so content, and I about to drop a bombshell.'

Brian pictured the sitting room with the stucco ceiling and the French doors that opened on to the garden. He saw the row of beeches by the boundary wall: a line of defence against the invasion of what Clare Duggan called the 'upstarts' from the new estate. He saw the bull-necked man sitting on the edge of the armchair as if in readiness for anyone who might break in and steal the fruit of thirty-five years' labour.

After the war, John Joe Duggan had mended punctures and repaired cars in a shed, while the wind whistled through holes in the corrugated iron sheets. With the help of an uncle in New York, he was able to secure an agency in the early sixties. In twenty years, 'JJ Duggan Motors' was sealed to rear windows of half the cars around the midlands.

'How did you manage to break the news?'

'Strange. She smelled trouble early on. In any case, she began to ask how things were at the hospital.' Clare had pretended to work at a piece of crochet and keep an eye on the television. Holding up her handiwork to see how it hung, she peered across at her favourite child. The questions started again: 'How is Brian since he went to that godforsaken place? It's been a while since he's been here. We'll have to invite him down for a weekend soon.'

'I knew I had to say it then or I would return to Orla as I had done the week before, so I asked Dad would he lower the television – I had something to tell them.'

His face grew tense as he recounted the details: the stunned silence and the muted canned laughter from the television, the crochet needles lifeless on his mother's lap. His father was the first to regain his balance and he fired one salvo after another. He sneered when Paul insisted that his mind was made up and that he had prayed about it for months.

'And you had seven years to pray about it in Maynooth. Wouldn't one imagine that seven years would be long enough to pray about it? I never had seven years to pray about decisions I had to make in life. You wouldn't stay down here when you were ordained: it was too quiet for you. You wanted to go to Dublin – "greater challenge", isn't that what you said? Greater challenge, my foot.' 'And I believe when the archbishop up there asked if you wanted to be permanent, you refused him. Do you know what you are doing at all?' He stood – and like a caged animal –, paced up and down.

His mother buried her head in her hands and began to weep. Between fits of sobbing, she pleaded with him to reconsider; didn't her brother, Monsignor Frank, often say that, many times, he had been on the point of leaving?

Her outburst fuelled the father's anger even more.

'You'll be making a fool of yourself and a laughing stock of the family,' he exploded. 'How do you think we're going to explain this to the neighbours?'

Paul stopped and looked away towards Howth. Far out on the glittering water two men were riding surfboards into the sun. 'The worst is yet to come when I tell them about Orla.'

'I know.'

A couple of weeks later, Paul steeled himself for the second showdown. The reaction was nightmarish. John Joe Duggan unleashed the strength that had enabled him to climb from his father's forge to a mansion that caught the attention of passersby on their way into Athlone. What pained him most was to see the woman he adored withdrawn into a world of her own. He always knew that Paul was his wife's favourite and accepted that as part of a mother's preference for the eldest; still, he thought it unfair to Barry and Niall, and had determined always to treat his three sons as equals.

Since the upset, he had found himself, at odd moments, inside the glass surround of his office, staring at the gleaming cars in the showroom. Motes of the past floated across the screen of his memory: the time when the three boys were at Blackrock College and she would take extra care with Paul's Halloween parcel. He never understood why they had had to go to boarding school in the first place; he had left the national school at fourteen and had never regretted it. But that was another of Clare's wishes, like deciding that Paul should be named after her father. And John Joe, whose word was final when he and Barry sat around the table with the managers in the upstairs office, never once opposed the guard's daughter he married in Ballinagar Church nearly forty years before.

When it was impossible to reason with his father, face to face, Paul took to phoning, but that too failed. He rang one evening, hoping his mother would answer, but when he heard the dreaded voice, he was tempted to put down the receiver. As calmly as he could, however, he appealed for understanding, admitting that it wasn't easy for any of them and that he wanted to make peace.

'Don't you think you have created enough trouble already?' The controlled anger caused the voice to sound hoarse. 'Do you know that your mother, right now, is upstairs resting after seeing a top psychiatrist up in Fitzwilliam Square? And those boyos don't come cheap.' He had to pause to recover his breath. 'Nice story I have at this time in my life: my wife on pills because her son the priest couldn't keep his trousers on.'

It was a sledge-blow, but Paul, now near to breaking-point, persisted.

'Can't you see that Orla and I need your support, more especially at this time?'

'Support. You need my support,' he jeered. 'I never thought I'd see the day when a son of mine would go back on a promise he made on his knees before the bishop. I never thought I'd see that day.' Afraid he might be heard upstairs, he lowered his voice and hissed: 'Don't attempt to look for sympathy from me or from your mother for what you have done. And by the way,' he delivered the knockout punch before hanging up, 'don't mention that whore's name in my presence again.'

During the summer, Paul resigned from the priesthood. He and Orla had already found a flat in Elgin Road. In the autumn he would return to university and do postgraduate studies in psychology; meanwhile he searched for a job to supplement Orla's salary. From half-listening to reports about other priests who had left the Church, he understood that the diocese provided them with a full salary until they became self-supporting. It was common knowledge that Bishop Roche, unlike his predecessor, was sympathetic to priests in difficulty. So when he drove beneath the arch with its inscription 'Semper Fidelis' and saw across the green expanse the gothic mansion, he anticipated a meeting where his decision, even if regretted, would be respected by this frail man.

A middle-aged woman, her glasses hanging from a silver chain around her neck, ushered him in to one of the side parlours; her manner was gentle, like a doctor's receptionist who knew something of the patient's condition. The marble fireplace, the studded leather armchairs, the picture of the martyred Saint Sebastian came to him like fragments from a dream or a previous life. Only the black and white of Bishop Roche taken outside Maynooth Seminary was new; even now the penetrating eye reproved him.

That dreaded squint had been applied when Paul, like every other student, had arrived for the annual interview during his Easter holidays from Maynooth. From the same reception room, one of the priest-secretaries led the way down the wide corridor, the only sound being the swish of their soutanes: a light tap on the half-open door and he was ushered into the dimly lit office.

The smell of ancient books drew the eyes to the hard-bound volumes that lined the walls, then to the slight figure of the bishop stealing from behind the desk, one bony hand on the pectoral cross, the other extended for the genuflected kiss. The whispered voice invited him to sit in front of the fire, while Roche resumed his place on a higher chair.

In the same room from which he influenced local and national politics with county councillors and even Dáil deputies, summoned down from Leinster House, Bishop Roche probed or grew silent, all the while scrutinizing every reaction. As expected, he posed the inevitable question to all First Years: 'Have I instructed you, my son, on matters that relate to life and the Creator's plan for mankind?'

'No, My Lord' was the sensible answer. Over the years, students had learned to endure the instruction on sexual intercourse and personal hygiene, and then receive the crucifix they would place beneath their pillow to ward off bad thoughts.

In Maynooth they still talked about Duffy, who had assured His Lordship with a mirthful smile: 'There's hardly need for that, My Lord. Sure didn't I grow up with cows and bulls.'

Apart from the upward twitch of an eyebrow, the face had shown little emotion. 'There is a vast difference between instinctual and rational behaviour, my son, between what the Creator ordained for the human and the animal species. Between', the lower row of teeth jutted out in a leer, 'the bulls and the cows, and the sacredness of human reproduction.' Duffy had to return every month that summer until he had been disabused of his ignorance.

A tap on the door disturbed Paul's reverie. 'My apologies,' said Bishop Roche's successor, shaking his hand. 'You know how meetings go on.' He gestured towards the other armchair and settled himself with his back to the light. Despite the boyish smile, he looked pale and drawn, as if someone had stretched the skin tightly across the sharp bone structure of his face. He was short of breath, though he had only walked up the corridor.

'If only life could go on without committees. I'm sure you have a similar difficulty in your work.' He shook folds from a spotless handkerchief to clean his glasses; without them, the face became that of an old man, who had lived all his life in places out of the reach of the sun.

For Paul, the informality was refreshing; gone was the huge desk, the black soutane with the red buttons, sash and pectoral cross, so he wasted no time in revealing the purpose of his visit. He knew now, he confided to the bishop, that he did not have a vocation: the fits of depression that had begun in Maynooth, the sleepless nights and loneliness had convinced him of this truth. His story was received with punctuated nods of understanding.

When he had finished, the bishop grimaced, removed his glasses again and rubbed his hand over his eyes.

'Father Paul, you have been experiencing the cross in your priesthood and I'm glad you have come to me because, in the final analysis, only a brother priest can sympathize with the great sacrifice we make. You know, of course, that this is the lot of everyone who follows in the footsteps of the Divine Master. I pray constantly for all my priests.' He replaced his glasses and looked across. 'Nowadays, the world is becoming increasingly hostile to the message we bring, but then there is a white martyrdom you and I suffer, about which the world knows little. However,' he took another deep breath, 'you would be very unwise to take such a drastic step as betraying your sacred calling because of a passing fancy. Put everything in God's hands, my son.'

Paul's spirit wilted; either the bishop hadn't understood a word he had told him or else he had chosen to ignore it.

'I can make arrangements straightaway for you to be released from your hospital chaplaincy so that you can spend some time in Saint Bueno's. It's in north Wales,' he heard the bishop say. 'There, guided by holy men, and with the grace of God, you will be enabled to resume your ministry.' He smiled like a teacher who has unravelled a theorem for a dull pupil.

'My Lord, I have already made up my mind.' It was now an uphill struggle as he noticed the lips tighten. 'You see, I have someone else to consider.'

The bishop grew rigid; he began to fidget with his ring. Paul's courage faltered, but he was determined to carry on. He told the bishop about his relationship with Orla and his plans for resuming studies in October, and wondered what financial support he could expect from the diocese.

'Do you mean to tell me that you are going to live in sin with this young woman, and be a scandal to the whole nursing staff, and everyone who knows your situation?' He planted both feet on the floor and gripped the armrests. 'I should remind you of what the Gospel has to say about those who put their hand to the plough.' Through the horn-rimmed glasses he appraised the priest's reaction. After another crucifying silence the bishop leaned forward:

'What about your call. Father?' Louder now. 'Your call that comes from the Divine Master. Listen to the words of Jeremiah: "Before I formed you in the womb I knew you and before you were born I consecrated you." It would serve you well, Father Duggan, to ponder these words before you do anything rash.'

Paul could feel anger rising within him; his heart was thumping, yet he heard out the bishop. Then he spoke: 'I have made my decision, My Lord. I am not going back on it.'

Lips pursed, the bishop stared at him. 'So be it, Father. So be it. All I can do is pray for you.' He raised himself from the chair.

At the door the handshake was perfunctory and, looking at a point somewhere in the stained-glass door, he sighed: 'May God help you to see the light.'

There was a crushed silence that Sunday evening when Paul had finished his account of the meeting. Brian tried to cushion the fall: 'Another priest was accused of not saying his prayers, or else he wouldn't be ruining his life by such an act of betrayal.' In fact, the bishop had compared the priest's leaving to that of Judas, who had left the Last Supper; but he abridged things for Orla's sake. She was sitting beside Paul on the couch, her feet curled up beneath her.

'Ah,' Paul sighed. 'I don't blame him. Rome calls the shots. He's over a barrel. Priests the world over are getting the same treatment nowadays.'

Outside the light had grown dim; through the barred window of the garden flat, Brian could see Paul's Volkswagen in the gravelled drive. Two girls in jeans climbed the granite steps; their country accents and bursts of laughter signalled the return of life to Elgin Road. Orla slipped her feet into sandals and went out to the kitchen; in a moment they could hear the sound of a kettle being filled.

'Do you think he'll give you any help with your fees?'

Paul shook his head. 'We'll manage without him.'

The following morning Brian woke to a dull throbbing pain at the back of his head. He still had it when he crossed to the church for the ten o'clock Mass. To avoid the strident chorus of the Rosary Brigade, as Dick Hegarty called them, he went in by the side and hurried to the sacristy, shutting out the dreary intonation, 'Save us from the fires of hell, lead all souls to heaven, especially those in most need of your mercy.' The ragged end of a superstitious past, he fumed to himself.

Later, to clear his head, he walked over the bridge and down to the small supermarket beside The Spanish Lady; on his way he met women pushing prams to the health clinic.

'Beautiful mornin', Father.'

'Beautiful.'

'We're in for a good spell now.'

'Isn't it great?' He broadened the smile.

Glad to see the supermarket empty because he wouldn't have to keep up the pretence, he took one of the baskets from the stack inside the door. He weighed some onions and garlic and made his way to the meat counter.

'Have you no one to do your shoppin'?'

He was about to resume the pastoral face when he turned to see Phyllis Jordan at his side. 'Phyllis, I've been meaning to get in touch with you.'

Every morning after he had said the divine office and zipped up the leather cover of his breviary, he spent some time revising his plan for the youth centre. Since neither of his colleagues was showing any interest, he knew that local underpinning was essential for its success. Phyllis Jordan was one of the few who hadn't given in to the received wisdom of 'Close your door and mind your own business,' so he told her his plans.

'Sounds good,' she said, 'but where would you get the money to do it up?'

He explained about the government grant. 'What I need is the backing of as many groups as possible. There's a fellow called Morgan after it.'

'Morgan. The conman?'

'No matter. If there's enough support, he can't hold out.'

'Oh God, I don't think you know who you're up against.' She cast an eye around the shop and spoke in a whisper. 'He has a mob behind him. Come down some night an' we'll talk about it.'

Even though she collected the parish envelopes and Brian had chatted every Sunday to her and her husband outside the church, his visit to their house fell short of his expectations and brought home to him the social gap that lay between them. He had a vague hope of dropping in on them as in Beechmount, where he had a circle of homes to call to during idle times: after a meeting, when it was still too early to go back to his empty presbytery.

He admired the Jordans' efforts to build a community and felt drawn to help them. Pride in their house, also, reflected a desire to succeed. The living room had none of the garish ornaments, the black-laced Spanish dancer or the bouquets of plastic flowers displayed on every television and windowsill. Instead, lace antimacassars lay on the couch and the armchairs. On the tubular glass table beside the television, a lamp with a green shade matched that of the standard lamp behind Phyllis' armchair. In front of the fireplace, a vase of freshly cut flowers blended with fern fronds.

Nevertheless, the conversation became tiresome and repetitive: how unemployment was ruining the area. Vandalism. Nothing but trouble. Phyllis would leave in the morning if they could get the money to move to the purchase houses in Greenoaks. She was sickened by the sight of burned-out cars on a Monday morning, the crash of broken bottles in the laneway at night and being wakened by the police siren.

Good manners compelled Brian to wait until they had spun out their story, then he brought up about the library.

'Do you suppose, Phyllis, the youth club will call the meeting? I could bring up my idea then. I'll get the school hall for the night.'

'All I can do is ask.'

The main business completed, Phyllis and Tony reverted to a description of Melrose. But Brian had had enough. He put on an act of stretching himself: he was on the morning Mass.

'Now that you know where we are, we might see you soon again,' Phyllis called after him from the lighted doorway. Over her head Tony's arm rested against the frame. 'You're welcome anytime,' he added.

The image of the couple against the golden background remained with him as he drove away. Instead of turning into his house, he continued on towards the Malahide Road; voices inside were fighting for possession of his mind and he needed to go somewhere to sort them out.

At the junction with the coast road, he turned for Howth. To his right was the sea wall, and a crescent of lights extending to the promontory at Sutton Strand. He drove until he had reached the summit overlooking Dublin Bay. As he circled the island of foliage, the lights swept a car, revealing a man and woman kissing in the back seat. He stopped, facing towards Dún Laoghaire.

Would he always remain an outsider looking in on others' lives? How long could he ward off the daily realities that pressed for an answer? In a few years' time he would receive another letter. 'Thank you for your work in Melrose... .' Now Paul had gone and the two weeks they spent in France every July had gone too. What had he ever meant to Paul, anyway, and was the game of golf anything more than four priests herding together against the sour truth of their isolated condition? Now and again the stretch of springs or the excited laughter of the woman from the other car invaded his reflections.

Seven

The youth committee was reluctant to convene a meeting when Phyllis Jordan told them what it was about, and that Terry Morgan would attend. They had been content to use the schoolroom every Tuesday night, for games of draughts and Snakes and Ladders for those who were too cold to remain beneath the railway bridge. But out of respect for the work Phyllis was doing in the community, they yielded to her appeal.

Well before the time for the meeting, Brian checked to see that the cleaners had arranged seating. When he opened the double door off the hall, he stared at an empty floor. He threw off his jacket and began hauling in stacks of chairs from the senior classes. Afraid they might flick cigarette ash on the tiles, he placed saucers at different points, and was tidying up the gym mats, when he noticed a couple of women standing inside the door.

'Jaysus, Father,' one of them called, 'you must be expectin' a big crowd.'

'Bernie,' her friend reprimanded her, 'don't swear in front of the priest.'

'Sorry, Father,' Bernie grinned, showing wide gaps between her teeth. 'I hear Mr Morgan is goin' to give us a chippy. Ah, badly needed.'

'I can think of better uses,' he replied and crossed the corridor to the staff room.

'Bleedin' snob,' reached him as he closed the door.

Pacing the room while he rehearsed his tactics, he was aware of footsteps in the corridor and the murmur of voices. From what he had heard of Morgan and his bribery, he doubted his own ability to convince the people of the need for a youth centre, despite their constant complaints about the lack of facilities. Through the venetian blinds he saw a Mercedes pull up in the school yard, and, in the twilight, children swarm about it. Morgan's head appeared: he locked the door and buttoned his cream jacket while chatting to the children. A mocking smile on his face, he removed a hand from his pocket, flung a fistful of coins in the air and walked away. Like seagulls for scraps of bread, the children dived for the money. Brian had prepared his strategy and was about to face the meeting when he heard the word 'priest' coming from the corridor. He halted. 'Who in the fuck does he think he is?' Morgan was saying. He waited until they had gone, then opened the door.

A pall of cigarette smoke hung over the gathering; at the top of the hall, the youth committee sat behind a table: one of them was leaning across to talk to Phyllis Jordan. Hoping that at least one of the other priests would turn up for support, Brian searched the audience; they were nowhere to be seen.

The chairman called the meeting to order. 'There's hope for the future,' he said, 'when so many are willing to give up *Coronation Street*.'

'Yeah, but don't keep us all night, Fred,' said a woman, tossing cigarette ash on the floor. 'I don't want to miss me Benny Hill.'

'Only one item on the agenda,' the chairman announced, and outlined the proposal from the committee: should they apply for a grant to convert the library or consider other options? He invited suggestions.

Before long, Brian saw that Morgan had planted mouthpieces, who were turning the scales in his favour.

'Yeah,' said one woman, 'all right for them that have cars; we do have to go to the village for a video. Be great to be able to run around, especially on a Saturday night and also pick up a curry.' The very thought had created a mouthwatering effect, so that a tone of longing crept into her voice.

When he felt that the night was his, Morgan stood up. 'I'll be short and sweet. No use keeping that woman from Benny Hill.' They laughed in support.

'Who's to deny,' he said, in a neighbourly manner, 'that a fish and chip shop and a video library aren't a youth facility. I'd have been glad of them when I was a youth.' He went on to assure the meeting that he would be talking to a government minister, a personal friend, who would 'leave no stone unturned' until Melrose had its own youth centre, as good as any in Dublin.

While they were applauding, Brian signalled to the chairman and stood up.

'Right now,' he began, 'while we are talking and maybe looking forward to watching television later on –'

'I hope you're not runnin' off to see Benny Hill, Father,' someone called from the back. He smiled and allowed the laughter to die. 'There are five boys. Five from this parish who are in prison. Every evening at eight o'clock they hear the scrape of a key when the guard locks them in their cells until the following morning. They are boys of sixteen; in my opinion, not hardened criminals. They got into trouble, wandering the streets at night, smoking hash under the railway bridge and then breaking into homes to feed their addiction.' He raised an outstretched palm. 'Five. How many next year? We are being challenged tonight. Are we willing to take up that challenge? The government will provide the money and the parish will supply the rest if you give it your support. Fish and chips, and videos, or your young people's future?' Water gurgled in one of the radiators. 'I'm not so foolish as to think that a youth centre would solve your problems, but it would be a start.'

'He's right. Father O'Neill is right,' said a man who had been slouched over the empty chair in front of him. Others nodded their heads and murmured agreement, but Terry Morgan was quickly on his feet.

'Father O'Neill is dead right. And I'm proposing now that we go home and think about it and then meet in a week or so.'

And give him time to influence others, Brian thought. He stood again, but remained in his place at the back so that all heads except Morgan's turned towards him. 'We can't lose any time about this. Either we are for a youth centre or against it. By the way,' he added before sitting down, 'I intend, with your permission, to make a short report on this meeting and put it in the parish newsletter.'

The ploy worked. For Morgan, gaining the library was less important than his future in public life; any write up which might cast him in a bad light he couldn't afford.

That night Brian celebrated his victory alone. Phyllis Jordan had held on after the others while he locked the school, but he refused her invitation for a cup of tea, ostensibly to make a phone call; in fact, he had no wish to hear another account of what was wrong with Melrose. Instead, he sat in silence, resting the whiskey on the arm of his chair and trying to control his racing thoughts. A mountain of work loomed ahead: setting up a committee, advertising for tenders, keeping an eye on the reconstruction.

Frequently in Beechmount he had phoned Tim Sheridan at that time of night, especially if he needed advice. Melrose was different. Counting the Sunday collection, the three priests had no time to talk about the pastoral side of their ministry. In the parish office they spilled the cash out of cloth bags and groped about the stack until they had sorted out the coins.

Soon after he had arrived in the parish, Brian received a warning from the other curate: 'Keep out of The Ayatollah's way at the count.' The eyes danced in the plump face: 'On a Monday he's like a bull in a pound.'

Brian laughed.

'If he's not playing cards in Muredach Hogan's house, he goes to his brother out in Raheny on a Sunday night. Maybe it's from seeing the family set-up and what he's missing that gets his dander up. Who knows?'

The wisdom of Dick's advice soon became apparent. Whenever Larry, the sacristan, set out the wrong colour vestments, he received a roasting.

'Haven't I explained to you that you check the Ordo? Look.' Father Brannigan thrust the liturgical calendar before the gaunt face one morning. 'All you have to do is check.' He kept stabbing the page with his finger. 'Red, white, green and violet: it couldn't be simpler.'

'Oh, sorry, Father. Oh, sorry. The oul' head isn't as good as it used be.'

'No, because there's no brain in there,' said Father Brannigan after Larry had left, 'I give him a job a child could do and the fool makes a bags of it.' The parish priest's tense movements continued until they had sorted out the coins and had secured sheaves of notes in elastic bands. Now, instead of sighs, he began to hum: that morning it was 'The Rose of Mooncoin'.

They were tying the cloth bags when Dick, short of breath, joined them. 'That poor dear who is forever going on about her visions kept me for ages. And then I had to go to the school; the Melrose thugs broke windows in Divine Grace again last night.' The blue eyes stole a glance at the bowed head and waited for a pardon, but the parish priest's tousled mop remained concentrated on the bank slip. He had resumed his humming, but this time there was no life in the melody.

'Will you two take the lodgement to the bank today? I've to go to the school. I want to speak to Bill Sweeney.' Father Brannigan's question was meant for Hegarty, who had responsibility for the management of Divine Grace.

'That bastard thinks I can do nothing right,' Dick complained when they were on their way to the bank in Ballymun. 'He has to stick his big head in everything. Sweeney is retiring and Leo tells me the other day that he wants to be on the interview board as the patron's nominee.' His fist struck the dashboard, 'He has some trick up his sleeve; but he has his match in me. I'm going to make sure the vice-principal, Alan Minogue, gets the job.'

Minogue was young, energetic and anxious to ensure that the school was fully equipped to implement the new curriculum. When the children from Davis Towers began to show learning difficulties, he consulted a psychologist at the Child Guidance Clinic, who recommended extra teaching resources for each classroom; the Department of Education would defray most of the cost on condition that the parish paid the rest.

'I've been a manager of schools for over thirty years and they got on fine without psychologists and their gadgets,' Father

Brannigan declared when Minogue made the proposal at a meeting of staff and clergy.

'With respect, Father, it is futile to compare the past with present-day educational requirements in a large school.' The vice-principal's voice was clear and steady in the tense silence of the staff room.

Sitting beside the parish priest, Bill Sweeney, the outgoing principal, who only wanted peace at any cost, cleared his throat. 'Well now, maybe we should leave that until the next meeting.' He leaned towards Father Brannigan and whispered in his ear.

Though Minogue had opposed him in front of the others, the parish priest respected the young teacher's commitment and saw his haste as a product of inexperience. He would make a good principal.

Parents reinforced his expectations; already they bypassed Sweeney's office and consulted Minogue at his classroom door. The previous year, Divine Grace football team had reached the schools final in Croke Park; four busloads went along. Their support was as much for the broad-shouldered teacher who strode up and down the sideline, as for the youngsters themselves. Through the winter, when school was over, they had seen him in yellow oilskins, training the team at the back of the health clinic.

The blow-up in the classroom, however, when Minogue opposed the parish priest on a matter of faith and morals, changed everything. From then on Father Brannigan vowed that he would never be in charge of a school.

The incident had begun in a friendly manner: parish priest and teacher chatted beside the blackboard while the sixth class went on with an assignment. Father Brannigan sought the vice-principal's advice about a boy who was getting into trouble with the gardaí. Given that his father was in and out of Mountjoy, they both agreed that he didn't have much of a chance.

'And, of course, it must be impossible for that poor woman to look after so many children, Father.'

'True.'

'Nine in a family is too much.'

'Yes it's a houseful all right,' the parish priest allowed, though the voice grew hesitant.

'I mean nowadays when there's no need to have such a brood.'

'Yes. Yes, there's plenty of advice provided by the Church on the natural methods of family planning.'

'To be candid, Father, I think that would be beyond them.'

The parish priest's head shot up at an angle; he fixed on a spot high up on the blackboard. 'Surely you're not suggesting that they defy the sacred teaching of the Holy Father.'

The son of a guard, Alan Minogue had an innate respect for authority, but here was a ruling he found insupportable.

'Isn't it true, Father, that certain bishops didn't fully accept the pronouncement and many theologians are in disagreement about it?'

The parish priest scoffed at the lame appeal; he felt more than a match for the teacher when it came to Church matters. 'You would know, of course, if you studied theology, that crackpot theologians who appear on television and mislead simple people are grossly irresponsible; only the magisterium of the Church has the right to guide the faithful.'

Alerted by the angry voice, the children began to steal looks at the priest's red face, but he seemed to have lost all sense of place. 'And people nowadays would be better off confining themselves to their own profession and not meddling in theology, a subject that takes years of study.' He stormed out of the room, knocking a copybook off a desk and ignoring the sing-song chorus: 'Slán leat, a athair.'

Before he went on retreat, Father Brannigan revealed to Brian the decision of the interview board; the new principal of Divine Grace was Brigid Mulchair from Greenoaks Court. She was vice-principal in Roncalli National School, but had begun to find the morning traffic a bother. A qualified musician, she was in charge of the adult choir that sang at the eleven-thirty Mass, and every Saturday morning she could be seen marching across the yard of Holy Trinity, followed by a cluster of girls on their way to the junior Praesidium of the Legion of Mary.

The decision stunned the teachers. In the lounge of the Skylon Hotel they swore they would take it up with their union, the INTO. This was not the nineteen thirties. The decision enraged the parents also, and women came in twos and threes looking for the parish priest.

'I'm afraid he won't be back until the weekend,' Brian told them.

'Well, if he thinks he's goin' to get away with this, Father, he'd need to think again an' you can tell him that from us.'

'I'll tell him.'

'We've nothing against you. What you're doin' for the youth was badly needed.'

'An' Mrs Kirwan and yourself is doin' great with the kiddies' Mass,' another assured him.

'Ah, Mrs Kirwan is lovely and not a bit snobbish.'

'Not a bit snobbish,' her friend echoed.

In The Spanish Lady they made plans to send a deputation to the archbishop's house. Through a haze of cigarette smoke one woman suggested a consultation with the Minister for Agriculture. He lived in one of the big houses out near the airport; her daughter had worked there before going to London. Another round of drinks strengthened their resolve.

Yet when the school closed for the holidays, and most of them started organizing the recreation programme for the children, known as Happy Days, they forgot the pledges they had made in the pub.

Brian was helping Larry to prepare the altar for the Saturday evening Mass when Dick called him aside.

'Leo is back,' he whispered. 'I saw his car in the driveway, I wouldn't miss this for anything.'

Later the three priests met in the sacristy. Dick was about to give a blow-by-blow account of the reactions to the appointment, but the parish priest cut him short: 'Brigid Mulchair was the most suitable of the candidates and that was not my decision, but the judgement of the interview board. You know that. After all, it's you they should be seeing, not me.'

'Of course, Leo, of course, but you know how they go overboard about these things. They say Harding the social worker is egging them on.'

Father Brannigan stopped writing the notices for the Sunday Masses and stared through the slats of the Venetian blind.

'With her fat arse and the way she dresses in dungarees. When I was growing up, only men in factories wore them.' He finished off writing, closed the book and added with disgust, 'Herself and her development courses and putting silly ideas into women's heads when everyone knows that places like Melrose will always be the same.'

When the parish priest had gone, Dick rubbed his palms. 'By God, but Leo has done it this time. They're going in to the Department. A whole busload.' They locked the church and walked across by the laurel hedge.

Brian had intended to invite him in for a couple of drinks while they watched *The Late Late Show*, but, at that moment, he wanted to shut out all talk of Leo's strong-arm tactics; and lately, his colleague, though he fawned on the parish priest to his face, had become obsessed with The Ayatollah.

Yet, in his house, when he blessed himself and picked up his breviary, a jumble of images invaded his prayer, so that he laid aside the Divine Office.

His resolution to attend to his own ministry and keep at a distance from Brannigan, lest he end up like Liam Holden, was now being put to the test. He saw that whatever harm resulted from the parish priest's plotting would cause vexed parishioners to tar each priest with the same brush. His anger towards Brannigan had as much to do with the warped face of the priesthood he was showing to the parish as with the dishonesty of his actions. And the spineless antics of his next-door neighbour completed the bizarre world of which, like it or not, he was a part.

Eight

Soon after the children got their holidays, clouds, which hung like quilts in bundles over Howth during the month of June, drifted off; now in the early mornings a mist enveloped the hill and the summit rested on a cushion of fleece. Mornings when Brian sat reading the paper in the front room, children hurried past his house to the bus stop, clutching sand buckets and contending with each other's chatter to gain a hearing. Later on in the day, others with jam jars roamed through the high grass behind the sacristy, chasing butterflies.

To escape the fallout resulting from the appointment of Miss Mulchair, the parish priest slinked off on his holidays at the beginning of July. In his absence, the two curates agreed to an interchange for the morning and evening Masses. After the ten o'clock Mass, Brian mooched between the parish office and his house. He filled out baptismal forms for the children's allowances, signed Mass cards and passport forms for holidays in Lanzarote and Marbella. In the afternoons he weeded the flowerbeds and plants he had sown in April, erected trellises by the walls, and built a rockery in a corner beside the toolshed.

And all the while he knew he was clamping down on questions that ran counter to everything that had informed his life until then. School work had been an escape route, but that way out was now cut off. Parish visitations were impossible because those who could afford to go were on holiday; the others availed of the fine weather and brought their children out to see the planes taking off or caught the bus up to the Phoenix Park.

Following the programme he had worked out with Niamh Kirwan before the school closed, he rehearsed the readings and hymns each Friday afternoon. However, playing the organ and keeping control over the few kids who turned up proved wearisome. He wished for Niamh's return.

Sometimes he awoke at unnatural hours, when the sun had already lit up the beige curtains and prevented any hope of a return to sleep. The defences against the unrelenting probe were weakest at that time, so the questions he swept aside during the day now sprouted at an alarming rate. What was he doing with his life? Had all his fervour in Beechmount been purely an escape from himself? How could he have known at eighteen, when he wanted to make the heroic sacrifice, that this was the way it would turn out?

To deepen his gloom, he received a government letter: the grant for the refurbishment of the library would not be considered until the following March; his application was too late for the current year's allocation of funds. 'But the Department is commmited to the concept.' He cast the letter on his desk. Ahead of him he saw months of humouring Muredach Hogan so that he would continue to let the vacant room to the club.

In the afternoons he drove out to Sutton and wandered along the rocky shore. Sometimes he stopped, and with a hand shading his eyes, watched the windsurfers skimming over the water, liquid crystal dripping from their wetsuits, as they swayed and crouched to maintain their balance. Above the shoreline he made a grassy nook his own and, deaf to the whoops of joy from below, lay there squinting out at Dublin Bay.

Why didn't he leave while he was in All Saints? Others in his year who seemed cut out for the priesthood had put aside soutane and collar; they were now teachers or solicitors. One was a doctor. Brian had met him with his wife and children one Christmas Eve, laden with parcels in Grafton Street.

Over the seven years, the seminarians' manner of leaving took on a distinct pattern. They followed the dean's instructions and did a flit while everyone was at study in his room. When the bell rang for the evening meal, the students, in soutanes and birettas, trod the wooden boards on their way to the refectory. Forbidden to speak in that part of the building, they stole sidelong glances at the open door and the rolled up mattress on the iron frame. For a few days they increased their visits to the oratory and offered prayers to the flickering red lamp for an end to the doubts.

But it was easy to rejoin the flow of seminary days: football games, debates and the occasional day off until he had lain prostrate on the marble floor before the archbishop, and any seeping hesitation was dispelled in a glow of approval from those who kissed the anointed hands.

Now the glow had dimmed. He raised himself and returned to his car. Dick's words came to him from the night they had gone for a few drinks after the Corpus Christi procession: 'Look, Brian, in the Church you can't have any illusions; take care of number one because they are not going to bother much with you. Their only concern is that you are there to say Mass and don't give them any trouble. And make no mistake about the people here: they will have forgotten us by the time we've reached the main road with our few sticks of furniture.' The face was whiskey-flushed. 'And they are no different in any other parish, no matter how popular blokes think they are.'

When he got back home, a note was hanging from the lip of the letter box. 'There's been a death in Melrose Crescent. They were looking for you, but I covered. Dick.'

He was in no mood for offering sympathy, but he went upstairs, put on a clerical shirt and fitted the plastic collar into place. Even at his best, he could never manage the words of consolation that flowed from other priests' lips: 'She's in heaven now. God wanted her for His own special reason. And she'll be praying for you. She wouldn't swap places with us now for anything.' It seemed to work.

'He always liked your Mass,' said the dead man's son-in-law at the front door. In the smoke-filled sitting room, relatives had gathered after coming back from Massey's Funeral Parlour. Women squeezed together on the couch and armrests. The men sat on the chairs, others stood beside the staircase, their empty Guinness bottles left between the bannisters. A woman rushed to him with a cup of tea and a plate of biscuits.

'That's the way I would like to go. Peaceful like,' said a man whose stomach hung down over the waist of his trousers. He drew on a cigarette and took another mouthful of beer. 'Am I right or am I wrong?'

'Good way to go all right, Jack,' the little man beside him agreed.

'Sure, and what about them that is left behind? Do youse ever think a them?' A woman who kept covering her knees with her skirt shifted herself on the couch.

'Jaysus.' Jack looked across at her, then stopped himself. 'Beggin' your pardon, Father. Would youse miss me, Florrie?'

'I wouldn't miss your snorin' anyway.' The rest of them suppressed their amusement. Two women had begun their own conversation.

'Me uncle's wife. Three heart attacks she had, but there was nothin' wrong with her heart. It was the fear of the operation that killed her.'

'Go on.'

'I'm not jokin' you. That's what the doctor said.'

The other woman made a face: 'I hate operations. I had me operation done by Dr de Valera. A lovely man.'

Jack picked up a key word. 'De Valera.' He took the stand. 'His father was the only man who could talk to the great Albert Einstein and understand what he was sayin'.' After a respectful silence he added: 'And he was exactly six foot tall.'

'No, Jack,' said his companion with the jutting jaw, 'I'll have to contradict you there. The only man who was six foot tall was Our Lord. Amn't I right. Father?'

Before Brian had time to answer, the son-in-law came to his rescue. 'The wife is over with her mother in Cabra, Father. Very cut up.'

'Yes. Hard to take when it's so sudden.'

'She'd like you to say the Mass.'

'Of course, I'll look after everything, tell her.' He shook the man's hand at the door.

After the Requiem Mass, the cortège did the traditional detour before halting at the house of the deceased; meanwhile Brian drove straight to Glasnevin. It had become a habit with him, while waiting for the hearse, to stroll through the cypress-vaulted avenues reading the headstones, as though the grim details, eroded by wind and rain, might offer a clue to the mystery of life. He read an inscription on a moss-covered Celtic cross:

> *In my Father's house there are many rooms;*
> *if it were not so, would I have told you?*

He wondered. Was there such a house, or did people want to believe that as a way of making life bearable? Was this the final rest: dark and still and silent?

He reached a clearing. Below him he made out a mound of clay. Over to the right a JCB was digging another grave; the metal teeth of the long neck, like a primeval monster, disappeared into the earth and resurfaced to disgorge the rich soil.

At the open grave he waited until he heard the crunch of gravel and the purr of the hearse; he unfolded the stole and opened the ritual at the section marked Final Farewell and Commendation.

He had been in his First Communion suit when he had stood at the open door of the family tomb while men from the village rested his father's coffin on the wooden trestles. Out of the late June sky, drops of rain smeared the inscription on the silver plate and he wanted to go and wipe them away with his sleeve. It was a good sign, they said, for rain to fall on a coffin; they had a rhyme, something like:

> *Happy is the bride that the sun shines on;*
> *happy is the corpse that the rain falls on.*

But it was all happening so quickly and was beyond his understanding. The parish priest read strange words out of a prayer book, and the curate, a younger man, opened an umbrella and brought him beneath its shelter. Grown-ups shook his hand, bent low and whispered: 'Your father is in heaven with the angels, Brian, and he is praying for you.'

Jack O'Neill had faded out of life as he had faded out of his son's memory. Always cheerful despite poor health, he was well into his middle years when he had married Delia Hannon. Waiting for Hartnett's Select Bar and Lounge to open after Mass, locals had sniggered that Jacko had taken on a slip of a schoolgirl from across the hill.

The following morning while giving out Communion, Brian noticed Niamh Kirwan in a blue dress, half-way down the church. Afterwards, she waited in her car, and when he emerged from the side door, she put on a pair of sunglasses.

'The very man,' she said, opening her handbag. 'Will you sign a few Mass cards. I've had them for ages.'

To someone who didn't know her well, she looked as cheerful as ever; not so to Brian.

'If you're not rushed,' he suggested, 'would you like a cup of coffee?'

'I'd like that.'

In the presbytery, he noticed the strain, but put it down to a late night, or that time of the month. Despite his attempts to tease, her gestures remained nervous; every so often she kept adjusting the sunglasses.

He made another attempt: 'No wonder this country is in bad shape with teachers heading off for most of the summer.' Instead of the hoped for response, she inclined her head. A lock of wavy hair fell over her forehead and hung there unheeded.

'What's wrong, Niamh?' He leaned forward in the chair.

'You saw what he's like, the night you came for dinner.'

She was reluctant to speak of her husband – felt she was exposing what was private – yet if she didn't talk to someone, she would go mad.

The night before, they had clashed over Sonya's wanting to go with her college friends to England for the summer. ' "My daughter doesn't need to work in any factory; what would they say in the yacht club?" ' She mimicked his outburst. 'The real reason is he doesn't trust her and he sees every young fellow as a potential seducer. He was far from being a saint himself.'

She spoke to the cup in her lap. 'This might seem crazy to you, but I don't like the way I catch him looking at her at times. I know she was always special to him. This is different. Do you think I'm being neurotic?'

He was out of his depth, but he reassured her. 'No. No, not at all, Niamh. But then sure all fathers are close to their daughters. Like mothers with their sons.'

'And now our GP has referred Andrea to a psychiatrist about her weight. "Comfort eating", the psychiatrist called it.'

Eventually, she removed the glasses, revealing the mark left by Kirwan's rage. 'He shouted that I had kept the girls apart from him and when he swung his open hand... .' She searched her handbag for a tissue. 'To be truthful I don't think he meant to connect.' Her story told, she grew silent, and after a while, raised her head and put on a brave smile. 'It doesn't seem as awful when you confide in someone.'

'I'm glad. And anytime you want to talk, you know where I am.' On the way out she noticed his piano through the open door of the dining room. 'A Bechstein.'

'Would you care to try it?'

'Maybe another time.' Yet she stood at the piano, running her fingers along the keys. Instinctively, the five-finger exercise moulded into a melody; he moved to her side.

'Right,' he grinned, 'one, two,' and playing an octave above, harmonized 'Forgotten Dreams' with her.

When she had gone, he gathered the cups and was about to take the tray into the kitchen when he noticed the Mass cards on the couch, and became aware of the scent of her perfume lingering in the house. Likewise, when on parish vistation, a wedding photograph or a pair of high heels thrown beneath a table would put him in mind of his gaping need. And despite his effort to hush the inner voice, it whispered 'home' and 'laughter' in his ear.

Helping people to relate to each other is a priest's real work, rather than going around like a rent man with family-offering envelopes, he reflected. He was glad to be of assistance to Niamh; the weekend courses on marriage guidance were proving their use. His ability to relieve her distress too was satisfying.

A few days later, Niamh was back for the Mass cards. She was wearing a red dress with a white collar and matching belt. 'Come on in for a minute,' Brian said.

'I shouldn't. We're having a few people out to the house this evening and I've to go shopping. I could do without a dinner party, I can assure you. Just for a minute then.'

'How've you been since?'

'Do you really want to know?' She fumbled at her wedding ring. 'Why do you think I'm around the school so much? Oh, I put on a bright face – I always did. Life and soul of the party. And they say: "How lucky you are, Niamh, you've everything. And you look so well." '

'It sounds like you are struggling in your relationship,' he heard himself say, just like the priest on the counselling course had advised.

'Love and marriage.' Her voice broke. At the begining, Shane had wanted to be with her all the time. He counted the minutes until they met at the Metropole where they had sausages and chips upstairs and then went to the pictures. In the long evenings they would catch a bus to Dún Laoghaire and watch the mailboat going out while he playfully drew her to him behind the backs of elderly people walking their dogs.

She was conscious of taking up Brian's time and made to go. 'I've never spoken to anyone like this and, to be truthful, I'm not sorry. I don't want to go back to taking Valium again.' They were still talking at the door when they heard the Angelus bell.

She rang a few days later. 'I'll be in the school collecting charts. Would you like to see a hymn book I bought in town? You might find it useful.'

'I've a meeting, but I'll be back here after four.'

He was back long before that, working at his desk in the front room, and scanning the road every so often for her car.

The creak of the handbrake alerted him to her arrival, and

his gaze remained fixed on her every movement: locking the Citroën, smiling to a passerby and smoothing a tress of hair as she approached his door.

Like many women who are conscious of their good looks, she was painstaking about her appearance. That day she was wearing a saffron dress with black polka dots. The narrow waist set off to advantage the outline of her figure.

'I'm surprised,' she teased, 'that you're not out on the golf course. Isn't that where all priests go on days like this?'

'Which goes to prove: never believe what you hear.'

They sat side by side in front of his desk, on two chairs arranged for a couple whom he was preparing for marriage. Her interest in the youth centre encouraged him to review the many petitions he had written to the different government departments.

'You feel like a beggar at times. It'll be next spring, they tell me, before anything happens. Something to do with the budget.'

His eye caught the hymn book in her hand – a welcome deflection. Together they looked through the table of contents and agreed to use some of the hymns when the children's Mass resumed in September.

She closed the hymnal. 'Sorry for burdening you the other day with my problems. I really felt you understood. Thanks.'

'That's what I'm here for. To listen.'

His reply cleared the way. She took up where she had left off a few days before: the *Fleadh* in Athlone when Shane had searched everywhere until he had found a street photographer. They got their picture taken against a background of swinging boats and a ferris wheel.

She had often looked at that black and white photograph: his arms around her and his laughing face buried in her hair. Like pulling a loose thread, one incident came away attached to another.

Brian's story differed. While Shane and Niamh were cuddling in the Green Cinema or slowing their steps when they passed The Happy Ring House, he and other clerical students had been celebrating a springtide in the Church, ushered in by the Pope with the homely face. All over the world, bishops and rectors of seminaries were drawing up plans to accommodate an influx of students. Under the archbishop's instructions, Byrne House was added to the main building of All Saints to cope with the projected increase.

She rested the hymnal on her lap. 'We had started going out together the year before. Strange how people stumble across each other. I was on the rebound after splitting with Harry Meegan.'

Like one giving a dreamy commentary on a film strip, she spoke: 'Harry wanted us to get engaged. Then I invited him to lunch one Sunday. You should have seen the contempt in mother's eyes when he broke his bread into the soup, drawing her attention to the dirt under his nails. A trainee bricklayer was just not good enough for "a convent-educated civil servant's daughter". Shane had prospects, you see.' She smiled at the irony. 'And when one became pregnant in those days, you were rushed off to the priest straightaway.'

Shane had played the saxophone a couple of nights a week with the Blue Aces, a group he had formed in UCD. They became popular at tennis clubs in Rathmines and at college dances, and the few pounds he got helped to supplement his scholarship. A curate who ran dances every Friday night heard about the group and gave them the use of the parish hall; in return, they played early, before the main act arrived.

Soon they attracted their own coterie of followers, mostly girls, who had gathered around the stage for the Elvis medley and the Beatles hits. One night, Niamh, in a red dress flared out by buckram supports, joined the bevy of excited ponytails. The saxophone player, aware of the attention, gave a special performance for his admirers.

Niamh's friend, Mona Whelan, now in Canada, nudged her: 'Who does he remind you of?'

'Who?' Her eyes glazed with excitement, Niamh made a show of innocence, but all along she had been aware of the glances in her direction.

'The sax player,' Mona insisted. 'Isn't he the image of Ricky Nelson.'

'A bit I suppose,' she shrugged. At fever pitch herself, Mona was blind to the signals from the stage or the sparkle in her friend's eyes.

The Blue Aces struck up a Buddy Holly song, 'True Love Ways' and not since she nestled in Harry Meegan's arms in The Four Provinces did the crystal bowl circle so freely and shower the laughing crowd with its snowflakes. It was the last night for dancing before Easter and she was determined to bounce back after her parting with Meegan.

(The priests closed the hall for Lent; they also supervised the dancing and, with a sawing motion of their hands, separated those who were moving too close.

'Leave room for the Holy Ghost,' one young curate used to joke; he hated the policing job, but had to obey the parish priest, everyone said.)

At the interval, while the dancers waited for the big band to begin, the saxophone player weaved through the crowd towards the pretty girl with the red dress and the Tara brooch.

'There you have it,' Niamh sighed.

In the silence, Brian was conscious of her perfume and the slip-on shoe that hung from her naked foot.

'What happened?'

She looked away towards the church where children were sliding down the roof.

'The crock of gold at the end of the rainbow, that's what happened. It was great while he was a teacher – he even did a night every week with the Samaritans, would you believe? That didn't last long.'

Shane Kirwan had aimed higher than the semi-detached in Glasnevin. He had no intention of teaching commerce for forty years and then retiring with a carriage clock and a marginal pension.

He kept a close watch on the business world, and the expanding Ireland of the sixties provided him with an opening: within two years the Kirwans had bought The Willows, without even selling their last house.

'I saw him change right before my eyes. It was dreadful. And

I was powerless to do anything about it. He was an addict – for power or money, I don't know which – probably both. The more he had, the more he wanted.'

She bit her lip and inclined her head, gestures that evoked in Brian a desire to shelter her from any more hurt. When tears began to stream down her cheeks, he rested his hand on her bare forearm: to console her, he told himself. They remained like that for a few moments.

Nine

In September, Brian resumed his visitation of the classrooms. Work, he still hoped, would numb the doubts that threatened to sweep him even farther from a mainland of belief that, up to a few months before, had given him security and meaning, even beyond the grave. The antics of the parish priest in rigging the selection of the school principal had been another assault on a world he felt he was leaving behind.

He convinced himself that it was none of his business since he had nothing to do with the school, and he tried to erase the episode from his mind. But whenever the coast was clear, between Masses or outside the church on a Sunday, Dick whispered the latest morsel out of the corner of his mouth. Only five out of eighteen teachers were speaking to Brigid Mulchair.

'It's all your man's fault,' Dick said.

For the sake of good relations, Brian nodded or forced a smile, but he had more than enough to deal with in his own life than to give time to the ludicrous drama over which his colleague loved to gloat.

At close quarters he was discovering a world that he had only glimpsed on his way from All Saints to the Pro-Cathedral for the Holy Week ceremonies: broken fanlights and the smell of urine from the dark hallways of the Gardiner Street tenements.

Paul's wedding also was on his mind. Occasionally, while watching television, his gaze strayed to the invitation card on the mantelpiece. He had never been best man before and the thoughts of an impersonal registry office disturbed him. 'Apart from yourself and Mary Donovan, the other witness, it will be just our families,' Paul told him. 'Well, those that are talking to us. Orla's parents have been great, but John Joe and Clare – no surrender.'

Paul still played the occasional fourball with the others. The priests who knew him through golf or card games lost no time in spreading the news and, as in the case of other departures, morning phone calls spiced up their day.

The rumours varied. One report was that his mother had had a nervous breakdown and that Orla was pregnant. But when curiosity was satisfied, they lost interest; anyway, the shock that followed in the wake of those who had left in the late nineteen sixties lessened the surprise in later years. And older priests had discovered an explanation for the disease: 'Too much of this Freudian psychology and no prayer; they would be better off getting on their knees, instead of racing to those weekends to discover themselves.'

On the morning of the wedding, Brian parked in Lower Mount Street and walked along by the high railings that enclosed Merrion Square; fresh leaves from the previous night's storm littered the footpath. Across from the Mont Clare Hotel, he paused until the lights turned green.

The scene brought him back to the time when he and other seminarians had cycled from All Saints, across the city and up past Leinster House to Earlsfort Terrace: always by a fixed route and always in pairs. Before they had left for the university, they assembled in the oratory to recite the prayers that would protect them should they catch sight of a girl's knee in the terraced seats of G32, the main lecture hall for philosophy students.

'*Averte, Domino, oculos meos*,' the stern-faced prefect intoned, and forty male voices responded: '*Ne videant vanitatem*.' It was all so secure then, as if the ancient language had a power to curb desire should it deviate towards the flowering young figures in miniskirts and black stockings.

Catching himself in a shop window, in his grey suit and wine-coloured tie, Brian thought he could have been a businessman on his way to work.

In the foyer of the registery office, the wedding party had assembled, and for a moment he hesitated between the doors, scanning the faces for recognition. Dressed in a powder-blue suit that made the most of her blonde hair, Myra, Niall's wife, was, as usual, gaining attention distributing carnations. A charm bracelet jingled when she kissed him. 'Delighted to see you, Brian.' She fixed a flower in his lapel. Niall stood on his own, adjusting a camera lens; Barry was deep in conversation with a dark-suited man who looked like an official.

Unsure of his next move, Brian glanced at the wedding party chatting in small groups. Mary Donovan, spotted him. 'It only takes a few minutes, in there,' she said, pointing towards the huge double doors leading from the foyer. A flurry of excitement interrupted her instructions. All heads turned to where Paul was holding open the door for his bride. Myra was the first to embrace them.

At precisely the hour when the big clock struck eleven, the sober-suited man opened wide the double doors and ushered them into a dim, cold room. As in court, a silence descended on the guests, sitting on plastic chairs arranged in rows. The official positioned the bride and groom and the two witnesses in front of the desk and, with the formality of a customs officer, placed the rings on a silver tray. He stepped lightly to the side and reappeared, leading a grey-haired man with a book.

The registrar guided Paul and Orla through the promises while they placed the rings on each other's fingers. He declared them husband and wife, and invited the groom to kiss his bride. A nervous applause followed. The official closed the book and congratulated the newly married couple. The ceremony had taken eight minutes.

The reception was held out beyond Islandbridge. As a former member of the rowing team, Barry had been able to secure the Trinity Boat Clubhouse for the evening.

Every room and hallway of the wooden premises was crowded. At the centre of the function room, tables set in a T-formation were laden with trays of salmon garnished with lemon and tomatoes, slices of cold meat, and wooden bowls of mixed salad; across the top, bottles of champagne, wine and spirits stood beside trays filled with glasses. Those who couldn't reach the table received, over the heads of others, full plates and cutlery wrapped in red serviettes. Window ledges became rest places for wine glasses; nurses and their boyfriends sat on the stairs, balancing plates on their laps while they ate.

During dessert, Brian tapped a wine glass with a teaspoon as Paul and Orla, holding hands, rose and stood behind the wedding cake. They waited until a hush spread to other rooms before they performed the ritual cutting; necks craned from doorways as Paul thanked everyone who had come to celebrate with him and his wife. Orla's few words were inaudible at the back of the room.

Brian was aware of the couple's wish to be brief. 'I know that the presence of so many friends is a great support for Orla and Paul. Without wishing to entrap a captive audience into listening to a sermon, all I will say is that we are celebrating this evening the central message of the Gospel: the freedom to love. A love that is all the more precious when it is bought at a high price.' He raised his glass and wished the couple 'Health, prosperity and length of days.'

To clear his head, he went outside and rested his drink on the wooden veranda. Darkness was falling over the Liffey, and across in the Phoenix Park bare branches formed a tracery of veins against the sky.

'Well-chosen words, Brian.' Looby had stolen up on him. 'Great view,' he said, and without waiting for a comment, lowered his voice. 'How did it go today? I've never been to one of them.'

'The ceremony?'

'I believe it's like a train station.'

'No. In fact, it was done quite well.'

'Pity the parents didn't show.' He leaned on the parapet. 'Wouldn't you think in this day and age they would show some cop-on?'

'It seems they had made holiday plans months ago with another couple and they couldn't cancel; they're off on a cruise.' It was only half-true. They had had plenty of time to cancel and Brian knew that Looby didn't believe him. Anyhow, before the evening was out, he would have winkled out the truth from someone else.

Before the dancing started, Brian had a drink with Niall.

'The Kildare Street scene is not your regular stamping ground, Brian.'

'My first time.'

'Shoddy treatment.' He was flushed and glassy-eyed. 'After all the work he did as a priest, now he is banned from a Church wedding.'

'No hope of laicization, I suppose.'

'He got someone to speak to the cardinal in Rome who deals with these matters. You know what the answer was? "We didn't leave him. He left us." '

'That's the way they are.'

Niall drew on a cigar, 'As you may know, I said goodbye to the Church long ago, but I still think it's an appalling way to treat someone.'

On the way home, images from the day kept eddying in Brian's head: Paul's arm around Orla's waist when they stood side by side to say the few words of thanks; the nurses from the hospital and their boyfriends swaying to the music; and the dark huddle of priests who watched from the safety of the veranda. Still, he wiped clean these images and held fast to the programme he had set for himself: by the following spring he would have visited the seven hundred houses allotted to him.

The anodyne he applied to kill the pain of doubt shaped the pattern of his days; by night-time he was exhausted and sat slumped in his chair, a glass of whiskey at his elbow. Sometimes it was long after midnight when he switched off the lights and dragged his feet up the stairs.

Before Christmas every year, he had organized an ecumenical service in Beechmount. Initially, Tim Sheridan had been against it; inherited prejudice propelled the knee-jerk reaction: 'Those bloody Protestants took the best of everything in this country.' He relented, however, and before the congregation had joined the choir for the final *Adeste Fideles*, he had stepped up to the lectern to deliver the same words of praise: how great an occasion it was and how delighted he was to welcome the Reverend Mr Crawford and his congregation from the parish of St John. Beside the Jesse tree, the rector with the mane of white hair and aristocratic smile nodded benevolence.

At the November Divide, when the altar list of the dead stipends had been distributed, Brian suggested an ecumenical service.

The parish priest scoffed: 'Do you think you'll be able to find many Protestants down in Melrose?'

Dick chuckled in appreciation of the put-down, but then attempted to placate his colleague: 'Sure, can't we discuss it at the next meeting?'

'You need five or six weeks at least to organize an ecumenical service,' Brian snapped, 'otherwise you would have a pantomime.'

Father Brannigan put it all beyond debate. 'I've enough on my plate at the moment. I've been chasing after that bloody builder to get him to repair the roof after those brats from Davis Towers. Someone has to do the dirty work around here or else we won't have a church to say Mass in, never mind an ecumenical service.'

Over lunch in the Marine, tempers cooled and the conversation drifted from priests who had retired or died to the dwindling numbers in All Saints. Brian thought it as well to join in, despite his earlier annoyance.

'The new wing they put up while I was there is used for offices now, I believe.'

In a solemn tone, Father Brannigan revealed that His Grace was very disturbed about the number of letters he had received concerning priests who were drinking and carrying on with women.

Dick cleared his throat. 'But sure that's nothing new, Leo. Hasn't that been going on for centuries? What about MacEntaggart, MacAnaspey?'

'Yes, but the scandal of it.'

'Oh, the scandal, of course,' Dick conceded, shifting his glance. 'They would be better off leaving, amn't I right, Brian?'

'I don't know.' He refused to be drawn into the fawning act.

'Well I do,' the parish priest asserted. 'Some of the bucks that leave bring trouble on themselves. For the life of me I can't understand why they won't wear their collars.' Bent over the plate, he assaulted his lunch with greater intensity. 'I've seen them at retreats. They go around like layabouts you'd see hanging outside the Labour Exchange in Gardiner Street.'

'Ah, Leo, you're being a bit extreme.' Dick gave a little laugh. The parish priest ignored him. 'When they betray their priesthood and run off with the first girl that takes their fancy, they expect the Holy Father's blessing.'

Brian tumbled to what was lurking behind the bad temper: Leo must have heard about Paul's wedding in Kildare Street. He couldn't keep silent any longer. 'I expect God is more forgiving than mere humans.'

'Yes.' Father Brannigan reacted like a whiplash. 'That is exactly what this age suffers from: the sin of presumption.'

With a wary shake of his head, Dick dissuaded Brian from pursuing the argument.

Before the meeting that day, Father Brannigan had been at ease with the world; his latest booklet, *Benevolent and Charitable Institutions of the Archdiocese*, was in its final draft. His junior curate, however, had irritated him. Nevertheless, over coffee, he relaxed and, again, revisited a world where he was safe: his own parish. Our Lady of Good Counsel had built the finest church and schools in Dublin when money was in short supply and there was a ration book on every sideboard. 'But priests were willing to get off their backsides in those days.' During the holidays from All Saints, he used to help with the organization of carnivals, circuses and bazaars.

'And I was there the evening Movita appeared in the circus tent. Packed it was. Half-way through the performance, out she comes with Jack Doyle and one of the curates who had heard they were staying in the Gresham and had cajoled them. Of course, they did their party piece: "South of the Border, down Mexico Way." To see Doyle under the spotlight, God, he was a fine figure of a man.' After the show everyone had cheered as the couple went off in a white Cadillac with the roof folded down.

'Those were the days, Leo,' said Dick, winking at Brian.

On the feast of the Immaculate Conception, Brian said the evening Mass; afterwards, through the driving sleet, he hurried to the presbytery. On his way, Christmas tree lights in St Mary's Nursing Home winked at him from across the park. He groaned. They were expecting him at the annual party. He considered phoning and began to phrase his regrets: 'You know what it's like in a priest's life. Time is never your own.' They would accept that; people still believed the priest was run off his feet. But the lie cut against the grain; he would, at least, make an appearance.

The organizers were collecting soup dishes when he joined them: women whose vigour contrasted with the rows of decrepit people at the tables. Above the clatter of delph and the clink of glasses, they called out to each other, lifted stacks of warm plates out of the oven, and, with their hips, pushed open the swing doors of the kitchen as if celebrating the energy that had deserted all those they served.

At the top table. Father Brannigan, the only one without a paper hat, had already started on the main course.

'What on earth are you standing there for, Father?' one of the servers asked Brian on her way to the kitchen. She laid aside the soup bowls and escorted him to a vacant place.

'We've a head start on you,' the woman seated to his left said. Silver wisps of hair around her ear betrayed the blonde wig. Her nails and smudged lips were crimson and in the movement of knife and fork, bracelets and bangles glittered in the candlelight. She resumed where she had left off with her bald companion, he looking straight ahead and nodding to the flow of talk.

On the other side of the priest, a frail old woman made a couple of attempts to join in but failed.

'I don't think we've met.' Brian took her bony hand in his. From sitting next to the bride's mother at receptions and staring down a two-hour tunnel of small talk, he had discovered that most people are ready to tell their life story at the slightest encouragement. This woman was no exception.

'Six in my family, Father: four in England, one in Australia and me youngest, Josie, lives in Chapelizod. Josie is great to me. Father. The others too, they never see me short.' The smile faded. 'But after all, it's not the same when your partner passes away, now is it, Father?'

'I suppose not.'

'Forty-six years we were married and not once since the day we walked down the aisle of Berkeley Road Church did a cross word pass between us.' She leaned closer. 'To be honest with you, Father, I'm only waitin' for the day to join him.'

It was easy to slip into the confessional habit: she didn't sleep very well lately – a dog barking was enough to keep her awake until morning.

When the meal was over and the tables pushed to the side, the musicians arrived: boys and girls in a charismatic group, and an accordion player. With them were two clerical students, who joked and tripped around the room. The clerics were first on the floor when the music started; they shuffled around with two old women, calling on everyone to join them. A plastic smile on his face, Brannigan sat with arms folded across his chest. When the music stopped and all were applauding the dancers, he headed for the kitchen, thanked the women and disappeared into the night.

'We may as well not let them away with it,' Brian leaned over to his companion, now the only one left. Despite the protest, her eyes lit up when he indicated the dance floor. He led her around, careful that her arthritic legs wouldn't crumble; over his shoulder he noticed the woman with the blonde wig. The bald man's massive hand had such a grip around the small of her back that a length of lace slip was showing below the black dress.

Labouring around the floor, the priest caught his reflection in a full-length glass panel lit up by a surround of Christmas lights. The smile died. He looked an absurd figure bent over the feeble woman, the paper hat a ridiculous crown on his head.

A shout from the corner distracted his thoughts: one of the clerical students had burst a balloon and he, with his friend, was chasing another, much to the delight of the audience. They weaved in and out between the dancers. 'Great night, Brian,' one called above the music.

'Great.'

'Aren't they lovely, God bless them?' Through the fish-eye lenses, his dancing partner smiled up at him. 'Vincent and Damien, they come to see me every Thursday.'

'That's good.'

'And the woman that sat beside you at the table, they visit her too. She lost her husband last year and she's very cut up about him.'

Brian glanced at the grief-striken widow, whose two hands were draped around the bald man's shoulders and her head thrown back in laughter. 'Yes, I'd say she is.'

He wasn't due back to the parish until New Year's Eve, but he returned two days earlier; he had had enough of his mother's criticism of Donal's wife, Helen. As a matter of course, he had always allowed the tongue-lashing to wear itself out: not this time. The long journey back afforded him plenty of time to think.

Outside Limerick, clouds of gloom over the snow-capped Silvermines brought back to him the excuse made the previous morning at breakfast: 'I'd better return tomorrow. The forecast is for heavier falls towards the weekend.' Then the leaden silence. 'But I thought you could stay until Friday.' To lighten the blow, he rushed in with 'Sure Maura and yourself will be up soon when the weather improves.'

The two of them had driven around to see relatives that day. In the afternoon they had sat for a while in the car and watched the waves thundering against the rocks in Ballyheigue, but, no matter how much he tried to steer clear of family concerns, she returned to Helen. 'You should see her face if he forgets to remove his Wellingtons before he comes inside the back door, and, of course, she had to throw out a perfectly good set of presses and demand the most modern kitchen, as you saw.'

All she needed was a murmur of agreement and she was off again. 'The very minute she got holidays from the school, do you think she would raise a hand to help him? And wait until you hear the latest: she is now complaining of stress and saying that she will give up teaching altogether. Little she knows about stress.'

'It's getting a bit cold, Mam,' he said, shifting behind the steering wheel. 'Will we drive to Tralee and have a cup of coffee?'

On the way she took up her theme again: 'She was off every night last summer and he up in the fields until dark cutting silage.'

As he switched on the wipers to clear the windscreen of sleet, he pictured his mother: a solitary figure in the two-room extension, built by Donal to satisfy his wife. Beside her on a table the RTÉ Guide and, on a shelf beneath, a bundle of Mills and Boon novelettes. She no longer seemed interested in selecting a record from the collection that included all the great composers. Once he used to love watching her expression change when she listened to music, as if she had been transported to another world. She had introduced him to Mozart, Beethoven and Verdi and had given him his first piano lessons. And when the parish clerk got sick, just before the Confirmations, the priest visited the school and asked for a volunteer to serve the bishop's Mass. Brian put up his hand and in two weeks his mother had taught him the Latin responses. Mother and son did a last dry run together: she spoke the words of the bishop, he responded without a single mistake. 'You'll do fine tomorrow,' she rewarded him. 'And sure, maybe you'll say Mass yourself one day.'

A spasm of guilt gripped him; he should have stayed a while longer. But he was weary. He was weary too of Donal's single interest: the drop in cattle prices and how the farmers were crippled with tax, and the bank repayments he'd had to make since buying Deenihan's place. The recital was convincing until he had taken a walk down by the farmyard and seen the vast herd milling around the silage feeder, a cloud of steam rising from their wide backs. He stood overlooking the sloping fields and Deenihan's beyond the river: one unbroken stretch almost to the village.

On New Year's Eve, Dick dropped in to wish his neighbour the compliments of the season. 'And by the way,' he turned on the doorstep, 'any chance you'd look after tonight's devotions for me? The Ayatollah asked me before he went off, but I have to visit an aunt in the Mater and I mightn't make it back.'

'All right, Dick.'

Miss Cummiskey was the only one in the dim church when Brian and Xavier, the altar boy, prepared for the Miraculous Medal Novena. In the sacristy they put a match to the charcoal: it hissed and spat in the thurible as it caught fire. The main door slammed shut and the sound of coughing reverberated as in a cave.

While he recited the prayers and led into the Rosary, Brian's mind was far from what he dismissed as an empty ritual. Staring through the crib placed in front of the altar, he saw a world where people were shaking hands and embracing on doorsteps, offering bottles of whiskey or wine in Christmas wrapping. His gaze fell on the boy with the short back-and-sides kneeling ahead of him, fingers working at the Rosary beads. One day he had confided to Brian that his only wish was to become a priest. Most likely, he too would climb the granite steps leading to the colonnaded entrance of All Saints, muffle desire that cried out for satisfaction and, after seven years, raise a hand in blessing over the mother and father who took the front seat at the eight-thirty Mass every Sunday.

'Will I open the church in the morning, Father?' the boy asked when he had put everything away and was waiting for Brian to lock up.

'No, Xavier, you take a rest. I'll look after that.'

'Thanks, Father.'

'Thanks, Xavier.'

It would be futile to advise Xavier not to rush into a seminary, Brian thought, as he watched him being swallowed up in the dark. Head bent against the east wind, Brian hastened down the footpath, unheeding the blast from a radio in the grounds of Holy Trinity, or the snowflakes that danced around the street lamps like moths drawn to light.

Ten

Before the school reopened, he had to sweep up the broken glass and take Andy to Chadwicks for wire brushes and detergent. Over Christmas the gang had sprayed graffiti on the prefab walls: 'Life sucks' and 'Fuck the law.' He was dumping the empty cider cans in the bin when he caught sight of Niamh Kirwan driving into the yard.

'Happy New Year,' he called out, wiping his hands as he approached her car.

'Happy New Year to yourself. How was Christmas?'

'Peaceful. And you?'

'I won't start.' She gave him a knowing look and then fixed her attention on the caretaker, who was wiping a door with a sponge, the froth flowing down the concrete and seeping into the manhole.

'Scandalous,' she said, 'the way they can't leave anything alone. I hope the youth centre will lessen some of this destruction.'

'There's always an unruly element that can never be tamed.'

For fear they would sink into a gloom, she changed the subject. Was he going to the tenants' social?

'I'd better turn up.'

'A few of the teachers from both schools have received invitations also. Anyone who helped in the community during the year. Alan Minogue and those. I'm not too excited about it myself, but I suppose, God help them, they are doing their best and life wouldn't be worth living if one didn't show. Like you, I'll put in an appearance. We'll keep a place for you.'

As he drew nearer to the community centre on the Friday night, he recognized the tune they were playing. Hearing the lyrics was like finding an old *sliotar* in a hedge, one that he'd lost as a child.

> *There's a boy, a little boy shooting arrows in the blue,*
> *And he's aiming them at someone but the question is at who*
> *Is it me or is it you? It's hard to tell until you're hit*
> *But you'll know it when they hit you for they hurt a little bit.*

Inside, the floorboards vibrated to the rhythm of dancing feet. A circle of women jived with one another, attracting shouts when twirling skirts rose, 'Connie, we can see your knickers!'

'You can't, I haven't any on!'

When she noticed him standing nearby, Connie called to the others: 'Youse can keep your eyes off him. He's my fella. Father Brian, me an' you'll have a dance later. A smoochy one.'

'Certainly, Connie.' He smiled back, remembering the evening she had sat cross-legged with her skirt halfway up her rounded thighs and talked about her winning the Queen of Hearts in Blackpool.

Bright lights flooded the stage and a row of red, blue and green bulbs around the walls gave the hall a Christmas appearance. 'All the women will be gone if you don't make a move, Father.' A man with a foolish grin on his face passed by, balancing two pints of beer and a tumbler.

The music stopped and the dancers drifted to the tables, set along the walls; in the clearing, Brian saw Niamh Kirwan coming towards him. 'You're late,' she scolded playfully. 'What kept you? Come on over to the VIP table and meet your old friend Muredach,' she spoke into his ear. 'I think he's throwing sheep's eyes at Brigid; you'd better keep them apart.' She was in a giddy mood, and, when weaving her way through the couples who had remained talking on the floor, she knocked against him.

He knew most of them at the table, except for Muredach Hogan's wife, who, with her husband, was about to give him a detailed account of their family's success, especially their eldest girl, who was going to be a doctor. The band saved him. There was a surge to the floor. Niamh was on her feet; she took a sip from her drink and came behind his chair, her hands under his arms in an attempt to raise him. 'Up now everyone. No exceptions. Priests too have to get out'. As her hair brushed his cheek, the smell of drink mingled with perfume took him by surprise.

During the summer holidays before he had entered the seminary, he had gone to the Ashe Ballroom whenever the big bands came to Tralee. Dancing came naturally and he delighted in the freedom of movement. At wedding receptions, women, out of courtesy, asked him out, yet feared he might stumble all over the place. Afterwards they said: 'You didn't learn to jive like that in the seminary.'

It was easy to merge with the crowd: everyone just swayed, wriggled or jigged around in the one spot. A set of slow waltzes followed, and while the rest were dancing, he joined the queue for a round of drinks. Later the band played another waltz. Niamh beckoned to him.

'Let's hope this year is better than the one gone out.' She squeezed his hand. 'I told you before; I don't know what I'd have done without you.' Driven by some impulse too powerful to control, he tightened his arm around her waist.

Luckily, the Harry Jay Trio, with a final flourish from the drummer, called for an interval: chicken and chips would be served in a moment, Harry said, and then they would hold a raffle for the 'very valuable prizes' heaped beside him on the stage.

The long fluorescent lights were switched on, detracting from the festive atmosphere and revealing the unfinished look of the grey brick walls, and the tables littered with empty glasses.

Brian hardly noticed any of these changes. He was on a roller coaster, quivering with excitement at the speed and the smell of sulphur in the air, and unwilling to get off, though aware of the risk. The drinks had made him heedless of the voice of reason; he was having a good time and, he decided, he had earned it.

A man at a nearby table saluted with his pint of Guinness: 'Youse were goin' well out there, fair play to ye, Father. Youse were made for each other.' Brian acknowledged the greeting by raising his whiskey glass.

At that moment, Niamh was making her way past a circle of men towards him. One of them put his arm around her waist, but she wriggled away. Brian missed what she said, but picked up the man's reply: 'I didn't have teachers like you when I was goin' to school, love.'

'They've forgotten to bring paper cups,' she said. He rose and reached for his jacket: 'Tell them I'll get some from the church. We've some left over from the bazaar.'

'I'll give you a hand.'

In the darkness their hushed voices carried through the church and, as two blind people, they inched their way to the sacristy door and then through to the office. The furtiveness of their act stimulated her playful mood. She began to whisper. 'Better not turn on the lights. That Brannigan has eyes in the back of his head, he might be passing by.' They were now as skittish as schoolchildren. Through the open Venetian blind, light from the community centre cast a striped shadow on the press where the cups were stored.

He stood on a chair and handed down the tubular stacks. 'Hold out your arms, Mrs Kirwan.' He affected the manner of a schoolmaster. 'Anything you say, Father O'Neill.' When the pile grew, she put on a show of protest, but he kept on loading. Then, without warning, she let the stack collapse. Some of the cylinders broke open, discharging their contents all over the floor. In the half-light, the scattered cups seemed hilarious and when he stooped to gather them up, she began to kick them away from his reach.

'Mrs Kirwan,' he pretended to reprimand her, 'behave yourself.' On hands and knees, he continued to collect the cups, all the while alive to the feel of her leg against his ribs. In one swift action he rose, caught her hands and the two of them began to jostle. But the jostle set free what each had been clamping down on for many months. They were no longer strong enough to deny the powerful urge; nor did they want to. He kissed her moist lips. His hands caressed and ran riot through her hair. The onrush of feeling almost engulfed him, but like someone startled out of sleep by a nightmare, he stopped, pushed her gently away and stepped backwards.

'Hold me,' she pleaded, drawing towards him with arms outstretched. 'Please hold me. I've wanted this to happen for a long time.'

He did as he was bidden, but this time he was wide awake, staring over her shoulder at the scattered cups, and half-aware of the amplified voice beyond in the community centre. Her hand fondled the back of his neck and expertly she eased his head down to her open lips.

But he broke loose, keeping her at a distance. 'No, Niamh, no. It can never be like this. Never.' In a muddle he set about stuffing the cups into the cardboard box while she stood, rooted to the spot. At the door, he turned, and said, as if nothing had happened between them, 'Let's go back. They'll be waiting.'

'Please don't go for a minute.' She approached him but he held the cardboard box between them. Her hand brushed his arm and then fell to her side: 'This won't make any difference to us, sure it won't?'

'Of course not.'

'I couldn't lose your friendship.'

'Let's forget the whole thing, Niamh.' He was already opening the door. When they returned, Harry Jay was announcing the winning ticket for the bottle of whiskey, and Muredach Hogan's wife was telling Alan Minogue about the old farmhouse they had bought near Lyon. She began again for Brian's benefit.

'We may even retire there, Father. I adore France, don't you?'

When the empty snack boxes and paper cups had been collected in plastic bags, the fluorescent lights were switched off and the dancing resumed. Niamh and Brigid Mulchair returned to the table and they all got out on the floor. And like someone who has a narrow escape from a car accident, and who manages to deny what has happened, Brian buried the shock of his encounter for the rest of the night.

In bed, however, he suffered delayed shock. He replayed every detail in his mind. The stabs of guilt he tried to counter with a forced logic: it was only a kiss or two and nothing sexual had occurred. They both had a few drinks taken. It wasn't as if they had planned it. He was making a mountain out of a molehill. He turned over, but more footage started to unwind. The sheen of her blouse, the pressure of her body and the feel of her lips were an adventure to a wild and exciting country.

Long before daybreak he was in the front seat of the church. Morning Prayer said, he slouched over the arm rest and pondered the previous night's incident. Unlike the tumult that caused him to toss and turn and consider outrageous options such as leaving the parish, his mind was now clear: they were both adults, she had become special to him, but only as a friend, and it would be stupid to ruin that by making a hasty decision. He would talk to her at the next opportunity.

He didn't have long to wait. That evening, ascending the altar from the side, he caught a glimpse of someone like her at the back where the light was faint. When he stood with ciborium in hand waiting for the communicants, he knew he wasn't mistaken. After Mass, he divested in the sacristy, not bothering to hang up the chasuble, and when he rushed out of the door a draught caused it to slip off the polished surface. There it lay, a crumpled heap. She was leaving the church when he touched her arm: 'Can you hold on for a minute, Niamh?' He pointed to Miss Cummiskey and another woman saying the Rosary. 'I'll be with you as soon as I lock the church.'

The anxious look on her face eased and she nodded. 'I'll wait here, you go on.' She gathered her white coat about her and slid into the last pew.

When the two trundled out, he locked the church from the inside. 'We can go out the side door,' he told her.

To ease her silent watchfulness, he adopted a relaxed mood in the sacristy, while he picked up the chasuble, tidied away the cruets, and put the chalice in the safe. If she wasn't rushed, he suggested, she might like a cup of coffee.

'I really wanted to apologize for last night,' he said when they were in his sitting room. 'Just so that we wouldn't misunderstand each other.'

'And I thought you were going to give me a sermon.' She

rested the cup and saucer on her black skirt. 'Anyway, it would be a pity to spoil such a beautiful friendship.'

'And all because of a few paper cups.'

Relieved that they had dealt with the indiscretion, and that it could be explained by a rush of feeling brought on by a few drinks, they relaxed into casual comments.

'Did the parish priest discover his missing property yet?'

'No, but if there's a sworn inquiry, I'll have to give the name and address of any accomplice to the crime.'

At the door she hesitated: 'We'll remain friends then.'

'Of course.'

Before he could reach for the door knob, her arms were around him. The scent of her perfume, the brush of her hair against his face, plunged him into the same whirlpool of desire as the night before, and cancelled all resistance. Pressed up against the wall, she abandoned herself to the urgings of his body. The avalanche of feeling within him, too, burst through the paper-thin resolutions he had made before the altar.

Inside the open coat his hands roamed her body, wildly exploring the shape of her hips, moving nearer inch by inch; yet, when close to his desire, he stopped.

'Don't worry,' she was feverish. 'You're human like any other man.' And, tingling to the pressure of his arousal, she looked into his eyes. But he withdrew his hand, and in the dark hallway they rested, conscious of the thumping of each other's hearts.

In the same seat the following morning, he made a solemn promise to the silent tabernacle that he would never again behave as he had done on the previous night.

The resolution lasted a fortnight. They began to meet in the city for lunch and when the weather got fine went for walks by the sea, to Killiney or Bray – a safe distance from Melrose. The hours they shared had to be thieved between the time when Niamh finished school and when the girls returned from college.

Thursday became their day for meeting: Brian's day off and also the day Niamh went to see her mother. Should Shane return unexpectedly from his office in Ballsbridge, she had covered her tracks by the visit to Drumcondra. And she always had an excuse planned when she rushed from the terraced house. 'I've to get back for a rehearsal, Mother,' or, 'I've to see Andrea's tutor in Trinity; he thinks she isn't doing as well as she might.' Her high heels tapping an upbeat rhythm on the footpath, she would hurry to her car and meet him, waiting in the red Toyota beside Our Lady of Consolation National School.

He wanted to show her off to the world: take her to the National Concert Hall or the Abbey Theatre, stroll down O'Connell Street on a Saturday afternoon. But that was impossible.

One sultry evening while Shane was off sailing, they tried it. 'Going public,' Niamh quipped.

Always on the look-out, Brian noticed a parishioner approaching in the throng and just had time to steer her into Clerys and wait there until the danger had passed. Like two fugitives, their stolen world was always threatened.

Once, in a Wicklow hotel, he heard a voice behind him. 'How is the new parish going, Father Brian?'

Outwardly calm, he looked around to see two women from Beechmount; they used to arrange flowers for the altar. 'Great, great. It took time to settle in, but I like it now.'

'We must have you out to dinner,' the woman promised while her smiling friend, in a tracksuit, scanned the priest's companion, and rested on her left hand.

'Well, we must dash. Bon appétit.'

Through the window of the Glenview, they watched the two getting into a black Peugeot.

In vain he wished to turn back the clock and be the one, instead of Shane, who had approached her that night at the dance. Often he recreated the scene: his hand touching the back of her red dress and the bright eyes looking up at him when he asked her out on the floor. Her fits of temper when she didn't get her own way, he censored for the sake of the perfect fantasy. Their love would never know such outbursts.

Dreams like this fuelled his desire for Niamh so much that, without her, his life would have no meaning. Whenever he was away from the parish, such as a mid-week break with his family, he spent hours staring out of the dormer window of his room, shaping her face on the plain below, and listening to the tape of songs she had given him. 'You must have a woman up there,' his mother joked at breakfast one morning.

During that time he lived at a giddy height. The clouds that had weighed him down vanished; he felt as if he had taken some powerful drug and was eager to engage in a hundred parish duties all at once. He took a greater interest in the progress of the youth centre now and visited the site every day.

One Friday evening, he looked proudly at the fresh girders against a blue sky, a reaction not lost on Lyons, the builder. 'You look a happier man these days. I told you we'd have it ready for September. When did you ever see a Mayo man go back on his word?' he called above the mixer. Weekend prospects led both men into idle talk about football. 'Isn't Mikey Sheehy a darlin' footballer? A wizard. I'd say Kerry will win again this year, Father.'

After their first love-making in his bedroom, a cry of ecstasy convulsed Brian's whole body and caused Niamh to enfold him in her arms, as if she were protecting him from the world. 'Brian,' she whispered, 'Brian O'Neill, where did you come from? O God, who sent you into my life?'

For the first time, he reckoned, another human being loved him for what he was. To her he was more than the face above the Roman collar that parishioners greeted on a Sunday morning, and then went off to buy the papers, or the deserving cause that evoked someone's pity after midnight Mass. 'Father, if you're not going anywhere tomorrow, you're welcome to join us for Christmas dinner.'

All obstacles to trust, like heavy chains, fell away during those precious moments when they rested and the fever subsided into strokes of gratitude. His life became an open book: the longing until he met her again after each parting; how she welled up in his imagination every time he caught the scent of Nina Ricci perfume. She threw back her head and laughed when he said things like that and he laughed with her and buried his face in her neck.

Despite all this, when he knelt in the church every morning before the Rosary group arrived, other voices haunted his idyllic world. These he tried to out-argue: wasn't he now working better, and Niamh's marriage didn't seem affected in any way? Hadn't he read a book by an American theologian claiming that it is good and even necessary for a priest to have a friendship with a woman?

But the effort to persuade himself was fruitless. He was violating one of the Commandments: Thou shalt not covet thy neighbour's wife. Guilt engendered since childhood compelled him to slink through the Saturday afternoon shoppers to Clarendon Street Church to receive absolution, and when he came back again and again with the same story, the old priest never lost his patience, but bestowed words of encouragement. 'I know you will be able to conquer this sin. I know it.'

'Thank you, Father.'

Good intentions chanting within, he would raise himself from the creaking darkness, slip into the back seat and in the cool dim church feel reinstated with the sacred emblems.

The Saturday visits to the side-street sanctuary were an ordeal, but what tormented most was beyond the power of the hand that blessed him from behind the grill. Relief that came with absolution was short-lived when the storm-clouds of guilt about the theft of another man's wife battered his soul. Disdainful voices from within accused him of violating what was more fundamental than any label moral theologians could put on his depraved conduct. He was sinking lower into the swamp-land of his own desire without regard for Niamh or her husband, whom he must have wedged apart; even pagan tribes in the jungles of Africa observed such basic laws of society. Only a few months before he had been arranging weekends for married couples, organizing Masses in their homes and praising God for the privilege of being a witness to their love.

He panicked when such thoughts ran wild in his head. It was like discovering that his real name and everything about him was only a fiction and now he was confronting his true self: an intruder, who had lived within him all his life, one who would trample on any rule to satisfy his hunger.

To assuage his guilt, he often checked with her, knowing already the answer she would give. One day as they lay together among the ferns in Powerscourt, he delved again: what they had together was special, wasn't it, and she was all the better because of their friendship, wasn't she?

'How many times must I tell you that you have done more for me than I could ever imagine?' She raised herself on her elbow and trailed a blade of grass up and down his bare chest.

'But if I hadn't upset things, maybe everything would be fine now between Shane and yourself.'

'You upset nothing. I know now that getting married at twenty-one and quickly pregnant was the biggest mistake of my life. I told you before; I was trying to forget Harry Meegan.'

'Why didn't you stand up to the mother and marry him?'

'It's more complicated than that. I was afraid she might be right about me.' She looked away towards the waterfall. 'You see, I was the one with "the wild streak"; my older sister was "steady" – that's the way we were introduced when anyone came to the house.' And when she started going out with Harry Meegan, she suffered, more than ever, her mother's nagging tongue. '"Exactly like your aunt. Do you want to end up in a council house?"'

'What happened to Harry what's-his-name?'

'He went to England. A couple of years ago I met him coming out of Arnotts. He wanted me to go out with him. He is separated now and said that if ever I was in London, he could put me up. It seems he has done well in the building trade and has a house down in Brighton.' While she spoke, an image, too tormenting to bear, rose in his mind. His arms went around her and he drew her down on top of him. Startled by the strength of his reaction, she looked at him. 'What brought that on?'

'I'm jealous. That's what brought it on.'

'Are you not jealous of Shane?'

'He's your husband.'

He was hedging. From what she had revealed, Shane was no threat, but the glint in her eye when mentioning Harry's name struck a nerve. As long as she was with her husband, he still had her.

'You won't go to Southend with Harry Keegan, sure you won't?'

'Meegan.' She corrected him. 'I might.'

'You will not.' He began to tickle her.

'You're not as strong as you think you are, Brian O'Neill from the bogs of Kerry.' She responded to the play; both of them rolled over on the rug, each aware that the wrestling was only a spice to their longing.

After making love, they lay side by side surrounded by a forest of bracken that hid their secret from the world. Niamh snuggled into the crook of his arm: she felt safe. She had felt safe too when her father had taken her on his knee while listening to the wireless. She had loved to sense his body shake with laughter at the BBC comedy programme. And in that world of trust she used to drift off until she was nudged by her sister to get up or they'd be late for school.

She loved Brian, a love she vowed secretly to take with her to the grave. When they lay together, it seemed good and wholesome; unlike the conjugal demand on her after lobster and wine in a Howth restaurant – the thrusting bulk forced upon her and, when desire was satisfied, the brandy breath turned away to become a snore of contentment. She had taught Brian a thing or two, but he was an eager student; the thought brought on a smile and she snuggled closer.

Though she had revealed more of herself to him than to anyone, there were certain things she couldn't tell him – being in love with a priest was frightening, and she felt more responsibility than him for what had happened. But she would never give him up.

A floating cloud cast a shadow over the riverbank; goose-pimples rose on the forearm that enfolded the dark head. Brian opened his eyes and studied her sleeping profile: the stone embedded in her earlobe and the hand, like a child's, resting on his chest.

Curfew time was upon them.

'What's the big sigh about?' Heavy-lidded, she looked up.

'The old story, Niamh.'

She raised herself, bestrode him and held his head between her hands. 'Look at it like this: next Thursday is only a week away. And another thing.'

'What's that?'

'I love you.'

On the way back he remembered the retreat.

'So we won't meet for two weeks then,' she said after a disappointed silence.

'Unfortunately.'

They waited at Sydney Parade while the train passed.

'What happens at those retreats?'

'We walk around the grounds of All Saints, talk about who's been appointed to what parish, who's fighting with what parish priest; we're served good meals, wine, the works. Then, after dinner, the snooze until afternoon tea.'

'Like a holiday.' She had taken off one of her slingback shoes and was massaging a red toenail.

'Well, you can go to a spiritual director and talk about yourself if you want to.'

'You never talk about yourself to me. You talk about plans for the parish or rows with Brannigan, but never about yourself. Why?'

'There isn't much to know, Niamh.'

'And another thing. You never tell me how you really feel about me.'

'Surely you know that by now.' He reached across and took her hand.

'Yes, I suppose so. It's just that I want to pin you down.'

Except for the times when he had to change gears, they held hands until they arrived back at Manresa, the Jesuit novitiate, where she always parked.

Eleven

On the following Sunday evening, he drove through the heavy wooden gates of All Saints for the annual retreat. As he cruised between the beeches, dappled sunlight swept over the car bonnet and windscreen. Where the avenue divided, he paused and swung to the right towards the football pitches and the farmyard; the left arm swept around to the colonnaded entrance. Across an expanse of lawn the stolid building came into view. He stopped and watched priests hauling suitcases up the granite steps. Others were tripping down to the open car boots, shaking hands and breaking into laughter; behind them, like a stage set, the grey façade against an orange sky.

It seemed a lifetime since he had climbed those steps for the first time, after they had made the journey from Kerry in the Austin Cambridge. Both he and Donal had taken turns at the steering-wheel. Then, along with his mother and sister, Maura, he had sat among the other families and the buzz of conversation in Marmion Hall.

He was glad to have Jer Quinlan when the moment of parting arrived. They had played together on the St Bernard's team that year; both opted for Dublin because Maynooth had more applications than they could take in. During their time together in All Saints the bond grew between the two students. On winter afternoons, when a permanent fog settled over the college, and the blinds came down, they raced after a sodden football in the back pitch with a few others beside the Tolka. The rasp of their boots on the concrete, and the echo of their contented voices beneath the arch at the back of Senior House, woke those above, drowsing in their beds until the four o'clock cup of tea.

But Quinlan was too spirited for the searchlight mentality of prefects and the Dean of Discipline and, therefore, left before the end of second year.

'You don't have the proper disposition, Mr Quinlan,' the dean informed him before the Christmas holidays. 'And your frivolity is unbecoming in a seminary.' Quinlan did an impression of the dean's mincing speech, but, behind the antics, Brian detected the hidden hurt.

That evening they went on the Long Walk, down by the river. Not a word was spoken until they reached the caretaker's house.

'Does it not frighten you to think what we might eventually take on? Never to go to bed with a woman. Never to know what ... well, what it's like?'

Brian tried to reason. 'Don't you think if we follow what we've been given up here,' he indicated the assortment of buildings beyond the soccer pitch, 'that we'll get through? I mean, hundreds have gone out of there and they've managed all right.'

When he lay in bed that night, he saw again the look of incredulity on Quinlan's face. And his mind strayed to the evening that Teresa Lawlor had waited for him at the railway bridge until the football practice was over in Danagher's Field. He'd seldom seen her except in the maroon skirt and black blazer of the Dublin convent school; that evening, in her cream dress, she was on the brink of high summer.

On the way home, celebrating an end to school days, they had talked about the Leaving Certificate papers. He rested against the saddle of his bicycle, inside the gate of the winding avenue leading to her house. Both were reluctant to break the spell by parting. Teresa was applying to St Vincent's for nursing, and, though she didn't ask, her upturned face waited to know what his plans were. In their anxiety to linger, the conversation became fitful: she would lend him *Walking Back to Happiness* if he wanted it. What did he think of Del Shannon's *Runaway*? And wasn't it great? 'The Royal Showband will be in Tralee for the fifteenth of August.'

Playing with the cross and chain on her neck, she recalled her last night in boarding school: how they had stayed up till dawn and had run through the empty corridors to the top landing, where they joined hands and watched the sun rising over Howth.

'Look,' she held out a ringed finger. 'We had a graduation Mass the evening before. Sister Regina gave us one each.'

He took her hand for a closer look, and then it all happened so naturally, as if bringing to fruition what was between them that evening. They ignored the topple and fall of the bicycle into the bushes. It was his first time and he thrilled to the yielding lips and the glorious pressure of her ripe body.

'You know I always liked you,' he heard her say, and felt her hands tighten about his neck.

Before breakfast, on the first morning of the retreat, he sauntered around the cloister at the back of the main building. Grey heads were bent over breviaries, and measured footsteps crunched the gravel path leading to the dried-up fountain. On the walls were inscribed, in blue and gold mosaic, the names of parish priests who had collected funds for the extension of the college. Alcoves contained the list of ordination classes; in one, he counted eight priests who had now left the ministry.

He was about to go on a final lap when he noticed Looby buttoning his rosary purse and strutting in his direction; it was too late to avoid him.

'The hard Brian. Did you emigrate or did the ground swallow you? You haven't appeared for golf in ages.'

'I've been busy, Jude.'

He was saved the effort of further explanation. Looby was bursting with the latest news. He touched Brian's elbow. 'I suppose you heard.'

'What?'

'About David Kavanagh. He's gone.' He let the shock take

effect. 'You remember he went off to Kenya a couple of years ago to work with the black babies and to find himself,' he sniggered. 'Well, it seems he found more than himself, because he met a nun there, a doctor, and they've hiked off to America.'

The two men left the ambulatory and followed the sloping driveway at the back of Senior House. They passed a group of priests, gathered around a gleaming beige Toyota; one of the group was informing his listeners of 'her many extras: power steering, electric windows – the lot.'

With Looby's chatter in the background of his mind, Brian was thinking over the loss of David Kavanagh, whom many hoped would be a bishop one day.

Even in All Saints, when he had been head prefect, Kavanagh had stood apart from the others, who reported every incident to the dean. Like all who were destined for promotion, Kavanagh had been sent to Rome after ordination and had returned to the seminary as professor of theology, although still in his late twenties. He had been an adviser at the bishops' conferences in Maynooth until his book, *Authority and Authenticity in the Church*, was published.

Then came the bombshell. On prize-giving day, the news broke: David Kavanagh and two other priests would not be there when the students returned in September. They had been appointed to parishes – Kavanagh to a chapel-of-ease in Wicklow. The archbishop, in private sessions with students, had probed until he had found what he suspected: Kavanagh and the two others had been teaching a theology of conscience and individual freedom, at variance with Church doctrine.

In Marmion Hall, the archbishop presented the awards to those who had distinguished themselves in the summer exams; then from the red velvet throne he addressed the students and the selection of priests in tonsure suits invited for the annual dinner. His penetrating eyes raked the assembly and fixed on the bowed head of the young theologian. 'It is sufficient to study the divinely inspired documents of the Magisterium and the encyclicals of the Holy Fathers,' he hissed. 'And anyone who contaminates impressionable minds will merit the punishment meted out to those who scandalize the young. As our Divine Master has said: "A millstone will be hung around their necks." '

'David, God help him, was a bit over the top, wasn't he?' Looby ventured.

'You mean because he had the courage to speak his mind, because he said what others would like to say but didn't have the balls?'

Looby backed off. 'You're right there. I didn't know him as well as you. Still, he was a bit of a loner; maybe if he had mixed a bit more. I find the game of golf great and the friendship of the lads a terrific support.' Yes, thought Brian, golf and bridge and leisurely lunches where priests try to relieve the tedium of their days with gossip.

During the four-day retreat, he kept to himself as much as he could, avoiding the card games and the nightly visits to The Cat and Cage. In the afternoons, when the blinds were down, he wandered along by the Tolka. The smell of YR sauce from Goodall's factory across the river still hung in the air and connected him with other times: glorious Sundays when nearly all Dublin was at the seaside. Sundays when he was memorizing Saint Thomas Aquinas' five ways of proving God's existence, and the wild cheering of the crowd across in Croke Park was breaking in on his concentration.

Returning from his stroll one evening, he made his way to the oratory for the spiritual talk, and knelt in prayer at the back. Priests in groups sauntered in, their conversations dying suddenly at the door. Most of the heads were grey or silver; a few had long strands stretched across the crown. One man had a plum-coloured crop right to the hairline. He believed that the dye, applied every Saturday night by the housekeeper over the kitchen sink, went unnoticed.

They sat until the swing doors swooshed and the retreat master's crepe soles squeaked up the centre aisle; everyone knelt when he paused with a bowed head at the foot of the altar. 'Come Holy Spirit,' he prayed, 'fill the hearts of thy faithful, enkindle in them the fire of thy love, send forth thy spirit and they shall be created.'

As one, the priests responded. 'And thou shalt renew the face of the earth.' With delicate precision, the retreat master arranged his notes on the baize-covered table and went through a hand-drying motion before announcing the confession times.

He had gained a reputation since his days as a theologian in Louvain, which was why Brian chose this retreat above the others. He would make a general confession to the gaunt-faced priest before he returned to Melrose. So far the talks had disappointed him: rehashed versions of what he'd heard so many times before. Still, he would keep an open mind. The topic that evening was priestly celibacy.

'Some years ago, while studying in Louvain for my doctorate,' the retreat master began, 'I was consulted by an American lady, a journalist, who was experiencing difficulties: what she described as loss of faith. I expressed the hope that this loss of faith did not coincide with her coming to work in Louvain.' A courtesy chuckle spread through the oratory.

'Before long she was finding any excuse to visit me, and had begun to seek my advice on matters unrelated to faith: her inability to communicate with her mother, the engagement she had broken off with her boyfriend and personal details of growing up in an Irish-American family. Then, to my utter astonishment, she declared, one night, how much I meant to her.' He stopped and fixed his gaze on some point above the heads of the students. 'My goodness. I immediately advised her to see another man with more experience, and gave him his name and address.' He paused, making a church roof with his hands. 'She never came back after that.'

'God bless them,' he smiled. 'Women themselves don't know when they are leading a man into error. And the mystery of the feminine mind is such that anything can trigger off the temptation. The sound of your voice, for instance, or even the hairs on the back of your hand.' At the end of one of the rows, a bald-headed man took notes, using his breviary to support the notebook.

The retreat master cited an incident from the life of Cardinal Heenan. 'During his seminary training, the cardinal was stricken with an illness and spent some time in the home of a fellow seminarian. During this sojourn in pastoral tranquillity, he found himself becoming attracted to his friend's sister; let me add that the attraction was mutual. Troubled by this, he wondered if he, in fact, had a vocation at all, and when he returned after his illness, he spent long hours in the college chapel. One day, he decided he ought to inform the rector of his intention to leave: his mind was made up. As he walked out of the chapel, he glanced at the statue of Our Blessed Lady. Time stood still. He remained anchored to the ground in contemplation of the gentle countenance. Slowly, as though a guiding hand had led him, he dropped to his knees at the prie-dieu, not praying, just beholding the image. His decision to leave wavered, then melted. He had found the woman he had been searching for. Leaving the chapel that evening, John Heenan knew he would continue with his studies for the priesthood.'

The talk over, most of the priests drifted out, and as they moved off, fragments carried back into the oratory. 'Shocking profound,' came from one satisfied listener.

Brian remained seated, unconsciously following the grain on the varnished arm rest. He felt cheated: surely in this day and age when thousands have resigned from the ministry, this man would have something better to offer than a story one might read in a Catholic Truth Society pamphlet?

He raised his head. The priest who had been taking notes put aside his breviary and let his rosary spill from the purse into his palm. He yawned, released a sigh of contentment and kissed the crucifix. God is in his heaven, thought Brian, just as He was for me once.

The red curtain hung in folds behind the altar and shafts of sunlight radiated a golden glow, recalling those evenings of early summer when a full assembly had invoked the Holy Spirit for the *ordinandi* and the resounding tones of the '*Veni Creator Spiritus*' had flowed through the open stained-glass windows. And when ordination day had arrived, a long train of seminarians in soutanes and surplices had paraded across to the college chapel to sit behind the marble pillars and wait for the procession of rich brocade. The congregation had stood in reverence when the hunched figure of the archbishop, led by the cross-bearer, entered through the main door and blessed each side in turn. From overhead had come the full swell of organ music and the choral salute.

> *Ecce Sacerdos Magnus*
> *Qui in diebus suis placuit Deo.*
> *Ideo jure jurando fecit illum Dominus*
> *crescere in plebem suam.*

Looby took the vacant chair beside him that evening at supper. 'You're keeping to yourself, Brian. Are you in training for Mellary or something?' He poured tea for the others from a huge aluminium pot. The priests were pleased with the retreat master; all agreed that he was deeply spiritual and that his theology was 'sound'. 'Did you see the way he dealt with the American wench?' said one man, heaping chips on to his plate. 'I was watching a programme the other night, lads, about ex-priests and their wives,' he leaned over the table to impart his secret, 'and you know, to see the wagons they got hitched to, you'd be sorry for the poor devils.'

But his listeners were more interested in the diocesan appointments, the bulk of which were made around retreat time and set in motion an itch of curiosity. Men, thirty years ordained and tired of answering to a parish priest's beck and call, riveted their attention on vacancies. Certain parishes, known as the Gold Coast until the archbishop had introduced a more equitable distribution of income, received special attention. These parishes stretched from Sandymount to Greystones.

'And who is gone to St Agnes', Jude?' A priest across the table held up a cup to be filled.

'Peter Kelly,' Looby informed him, and recited the list of changes from memory. Heads inclined towards him to hear above the din. They were still in a huddle when those at other tables were strolling out. Brian pushed back his cup and saucer and stood up.

'Hold on a minute.' Looby broke from the conference and

leaned over to him. 'A few of us are going over to The Cat and Cage later. Will you join us?'

'Sure. I wouldn't mind a pint, Jude. What time?'

'About nine at the door of Byrne House. Lynsky and the others will be along as well.' With a roguish wink he returned to the huddle.

In the half-light of evening, the wall lamps glowed in the upstairs lounge of The Cat and Cage. Except for a young couple in the corner seat by the window and a man reading the evening paper, the only others there were the circle of priests at the centre. The two tables they had drawn together were covered with drinks. Some were casually dressed, but others had pushed the strip of white plastic into the neck of the clerical shirt.

The list of diocesan appointments, circulated that evening in All Saints, was again the topic of conversation; but those in the early years of their priesthood were not affected.

Father Adrian Griffin, in a straight-backed chair, presided; he had a string of wisecracks that had the younger priests in fits of laughter. The scene was a replica of seminary days when The Griff had pranced around the ambulatory, trailing a cluster of First Years who thought he was a 'howl'. Even then, his ability to do perfect imitations of the college staff was well known.

'Who is gone to Immaculate Conception, Griff?'

'Cutie Dominic.' Griffin took a sip from the pint of lemonade. 'Dominic who?'

'Jesus, Cutie Domnic. The patron saint of altar boys.' The gibe brought on another guffaw.

They ordered more drinks and gradually interest in the appointments waned and Griffin's quips wore thin. The circle broke and they began to talk in smaller groups. At the edge of one was Austin Farrell; he looked strained and had taken little part in the conversation. Elbows resting on his knees, he sat hunched, and whenever the others laughed at Griffin's remarks, the sneer deepened. Brian was startled by the change in his appearance since he had visited him in John of God's out in Stillorgan.

Snatches of conversation sometimes rose above the chatter:

one priest thought the retreat master was excellent. 'Garret FitzGerald hopes to win the divorce referendum next Thursday, lads. I heard it on the six-thirty news,' another said. 'Garret can't even match his socks, never mind getting the upper hand with the bishops,' said The Griff. But no one was interested in politics or the referendum.

A tiredness had set in until Looby raised the subject of summer holidays. Broad grins and arm-stretching signalled the relief of two months in California for those who taught in the Techs.

'Nothing to it,' said one. 'You're supposed to be on supply, but all you have to do is say the morning Mass and then head for the beach or the country club.' Suddenly the group was one again. A priest with girlish features boasted about the white Chevrolet he and Jerry had, and he turned to Jerry for confirmation.

'There was even a small fridge beneath the panel; just put in your hand and take out a Coke,' Jerry said. 'American families really know how to look after their priests, lads. Isn't that right, Damo?' He went on about the barbecues and the trips to Yosemite and Las Vegas.

Lynsky affected disappointment; he would hardly have time for a holiday because of the commission work. 'A damn nuisance.' He tried to sound convincing. 'Not my ideal way of spending the summer, but what can you do? You can't say no.'

As the night wore on, empty glasses were replaced by full ones. The priests grew careless in their speech and waitresses standing near the serving area nudged each other when they heard words like 'shagger' and 'gobshite' coming from their table.

By now The Griff's audience had forgotten him and he began to stretch and yawn; yet, when he rose to go, his retinue followed. Soon after, the rest trooped out and down the laneway to All Saints.

Halfway up the avenue, Austin Farrell stopped and glared at the mass of buildings, brooding in the dark.

'A boarding-school for spare pricks,' he said and laughed at his own description. The footsteps came to a halt. 'For all the fucking degrees and theology, they hadn't a clue what the world is like or if they did, they wouldn't tell us.'

Brian went back and tried to calm him. 'Let's go and have a cup of coffee, Austin, or we'll wake up the house.'

Resembling a sulky child, Farrell yielded, and they headed for the small kitchen off the infirmary. Along the dark corridor, they made their way to what had once been the games room, but had since been divided into sections to cater for the occasional sick student. Through the wooden partition they could hear the rise and fall of voices.

'The poker school is settling down for the night, lads,' Lynsky said nodding towards the other room. He stood at the fridge waiting for the kettle to boil, and when the coast was clear whispered to Looby, who was taking cups from beneath the kitchen sink: 'Where's your man gone?' Before anyone could answer, Farrell appeared at the door with a bottle of Powers.

When the kettle had been boiled, they took the coffee and glasses into the infirmary and sat on the bentwood chairs. Farrell poured large measures, handed around the glasses and steadied himself before he sank onto one of the beds.

'The young guys are very impressive aren't they?' Looby, disconcerted by the silence, nursed his glass on his joined knees. 'It must be difficult teaching religion in a Tech nowadays. I certainly wouldn't like to be in their shoes.'

The remark brought a murmur of agreement from the others, but Farrell threw hooded looks across at Looby, who now became more nervous and chattered on about how young people expected to be entertained in the classroom and how one would have pity, especially for a teacher of religion. Anything to soften the baleful glare. The attempt failed.

'I never heard such shit in all my life.' Farrell growled.

Looby's mouth grew slack.

'All that crap about going on picnics in America. When will they ever cop themselves on?'

'Ah sure, you have to take them as they are, Austin.' Lynsky tried to rescue his friend.

'You don't have to take them as they are.' He now turned the stare on Lynsky. 'Not unless you're trying to lick arses and get noticed and maybe one day to be the head honcho and be able to piss on everyone then. That's the way guys get on in the Church. Licking arses.'

Looby gulped down his drink, forgot his cup of coffee and escaped to the wash basin, a look of fear on his face. Again an uneasy silence filled the room. Lying on the bare mattress, Farrell retreated to his troubled world. His head drooped to his chest.

From a safe distance, Looby made another attempt to gloss over the ugly scene. He asked about Melrose and how Leo Brannigan was getting on with Dick Hegarty.

'He has his match in Dick I'd say.' The panic in his eyes exposed the brave effort to smile. By now Farrell seemed to be asleep, so Looby regained his confidence: he recounted incidents from his visitation of the parish. Then he froze. Like a lion disturbed in its lair, Farrell raised his head. 'Looby,' he rasped, 'you're supposed to be a great man for bringing people back to the sacraments, and you fart around lapping up every piece of gossip you can find. Tell me,' he said, an evil look on his face, 'why didn't you stay in Wicklow?'

Looby was a cornered rabbit.

'I know why you didn't stay and you know why you didn't stay. Why don't you tell your friends why you didn't stay?'

The scrape of Lynsky's chair broke the tension; he got to his feet, walked across to the sink and rinsed his glass. 'We're all tired,' he said. 'Why don't we hit the sack, Austin?'

'Fuck off,' Farrell snapped, and kept his eyes trained on his prey. 'It had to do with certain goings-on in the sacristy, hadn't it, Looby?

Numbed by shock, Looby's face drained of life. Glazed eyes stared at Farrell from behind his spectacles. He turned his back and started to rinse the glass he had already washed and dried. Without a word, he vanished. Fast on his heels, Lynsky threw them a muttered goodnight and left without closing the door.

'Lynsky, you fucking self-seeker,' Farrell called after him.

Brian had no great love for Looby, but Farrell had gone too far. He was going to see this through, so he sat there, returning the other man's stare. After a few moments it was his turn to suffer Farrell's rage.

'And you, O'Neill, were always a smug bastard – yourself and Duggan, the guy that fucked off with the nurse.'

Brian had more than he could take. 'Farrell,' he said, 'what you accused Looby of just now was low. And a downright lie also.'

'A lie, you say, a lie. Why was he called "Judy" in this kip then?'

'I remember when that started – after he took a female part in a skit one time.'

'Ha, a female part. He was always taking female parts. He wasn't acting at all, if you ask me.'

'I didn't ask you.' Brian rested the empty glass on the formica top and braced himself for the worst, but rather than continue the fight, Farrell's body sagged. For a moment he peered across and then lost all concentration.

'What can I do?' was followed by a low moan. 'I get up in the morning, have my breakfast alone, read the paper, go to see if any windows in the school are broken. I go into classrooms and I feel I'm only disturbing the teacher. And the same with people in their houses: great to see me, but they couldn't give a shit if I never called.'

The lament had echoes of Brian's own story, but he adopted a nursing role and made more coffee. 'Drink it, Austin. You'll feel better.' He held the coffee in front of the drooped head.

Before he took the cup, Farrell wiped his eyes with the back of his hand like a child. 'I eat on my own, watch TV on my own. I have a stereo with sonic this and sonic that. I can play The Eagles morning noon and night if I want, but what's the use?' Bloodshot eyes stared at Brian. 'You know something? I was looking forward to this retreat; not because of this fucking place, but do you know why?'

'Why?'

'Because I would have company, even for a few days. The psychiatrist in John of God goes on with a lot of shit about my childhood and that I was too close to my mother.' He grabbed the bottle of whiskey, lying beside him on the mattress. 'Know what drives me to this? Staring at four walls. Listening to the tick of the clock on a Saturday night. That's what drives me to this.'

He let go of the bottle, and a wry smile crept over his face. 'While I was here, it was great. I'd have stayed for another seven years, would you believe that?'

The persuasive tone was unnecessary. What he had confessed resonated with Brian's memory of him: forever playing tricks. Even on the morning of ordination he was attempting to trip up the one beside him as the *ordinandi* in their crisp albs went on procession down the stone corridor. And he was always ready to join in if they needed one more for a soccer match.

Brian looked across now at the forlorn figure and another scene from his seminary days rose to the surface. The night of a Christmas concert: the darkened hall was still, rows of students behind the college professors. All eyes were riveted on Farrell, who sat beneath the spotlight, his fingers plucking the guitar strings and his flawless voice willing life into the lyrics of a Simon and Garfunkel song.

Brian heaved a sigh: 'Let's call it a day, Austin.' He reached and took the empty cup from his hand. As he supported him along the corridor and up the stairs, another shout rose from the card players.

By the time he had helped Farrell to his room, he was wide awake and knew the effort to sleep would prove wasteful, so after closing the door, he tiptoed down the stairs in search of the newspapers.

From the bundle in the recreation room he took both evening papers and made to leave when a poster on the wall caught his eye. It was similar to the ones they had displayed at the marriage counselling weekends: a little girl in a white dress tripping through a field of corn, the caption beneath declaring, 'Today is the first day of the rest of your life.' Now called the Centre for Affirmation, Byrne House was empty of students; instead, nuns, brothers, and priests, some back from the missions, enrolled there for pastoral renewal during their sabbatical leave. Others had come with combat fatigue after years of submitting to the will of superiors, and burying whatever feelings they considered to be at odds with the Rule of their congregation. A few were wrestling with depression.

He was up before the bell the following morning. From his window he scanned the pink skyline over Howth while he shaved. Pigeons cooed in the chestnuts and from below came the gurgle of a wash basin. They would celebrate the Mass for the deceased priests of the diocese at twelve, as they always did on the final day, then lunch before they all returned to their parishes. They had games of golf arranged for Portmarnock.

He hurried down the stairs and headed for the Long Walk. Out of nowhere came Farrell's desperate admission: 'because I would have company, even for a few days'.

At the handball alley he paused. All over the back wall initials and dates were scrawled, a heart enclosed; 'Shane loves Amanda.' Tufts of grass and dandelions pushed through cracks in the concrete floor. He crossed the stile and walked along the dirt track. The rising bell rang out over the soccer pitch, now a field of coarse grass and dock leaves. He would skip the final talk. Maybe Farrell in his drunkenness had hit on a truth: either they didn't know or else they were unwilling to face the world as it was.

At the iron gate that led to the farmyard, he stopped and rested his hand on the top bar. Despite the pious patter, the retreat had been useful: it had afforded him time to mull over what had been dogging his steps for the previous few months. At least he had time to make one decision. Whatever he did with his life, he would have to break with Niamh Kirwan.

Twelve

The morning after the retreat, he was cutting the grass in the back garden when she called. The mower had silenced her arrival and when he turned at the far wall, she was sitting on the chair he'd taken outside to say his breviary.

'I was on my way from the school. I had to collect a few bits and pieces I'd left over since the holidays,' she said when he closed the throttle and the engine had shuddered to a halt.

'Anyway, I wanted to see how you were doing after all the praying.' She removed her sunglasses.

'Give me a minute, Niamh. I just need to do the piece at the centre.' He spoke softly, pointing with his thumb towards the next garden where Dympna was hanging out the washing. 'Go around to the front and I'll let you in.'

He would be firm. The words he had rehearsed at the retreat had now become a formula. 'If we can't control ourselves, then we shall have to stop seeing each other, and if that proves impossible, I will have to leave the parish.'

No sooner had he come inside the door than her arms encircled his waist.

'Niamh,' he protested. 'Hegarty will notice your car outside – you know how he talks.'

She clung to him. 'Forget Hegarty. "To the pure all things are pure," that's what an old bag in Carysfort used to say to us. Did you miss me?'

'Of course I missed you.' He kissed her lightly on the lips, and, to free himself, placed his hands on her forearms. But she tightened her hold and buried her face in his neck. 'How much?' she teased. Growing arousal burned up his resolve and, instead of pushing her away, he enfolded her in his arms. When he eased down the zip of her yellow dress and felt her naked body, there was no turning back; as before, craving took possession of them both.

After the frenzy of their love-making, she rested her head against the kitchen door, a soft look of gratitude and satisfaction issuing from her dark eyes. 'I'll always love you. Always.' She kept repeating. 'No matter where you are sent.'

Failure to control his hunger frightened him now more than ever. Deeper and deeper he was sinking under the pressure of his own need. He was losing hope of finding a way out of the morass.

One evening he sat in the church, deaf to the rush of air when the door opened and closed, or the shuffle up the aisle, until Larry the sacristan whispered: 'It's gone seven-thirty, Father.' Saying Mass, he lost contact with the handful of people, propped between seat and arm rest, and only at the communion prayers did he wake from his reverie, with no recollection of having said the main prayer of consecration.

After Mass he told Larry that he could go home; he himself would lock up. In the sanctuary, he knelt at the prie-dieu and begged for an answer. The diocese had an emigrant mission in London, he could work there. The burden of guilt was becoming insupportable. He would talk to the only person he trusted.

Tim Sheridan was ensuring that the bees had sufficient sugar syrup for the winter when he noticed Brian talking to his housekeeper outside the back door. He replaced the roof of the beehive, and took off the beekeeper's veil as he strolled up the garden.

'Well, if it isn't the invisible man.' He removed the gauntlets. 'I called out your way. Children around the church told me you were "over there".' He pointed in imitation, 'There was some almighty hammering on the roof of an old building across the park. I went over but you had just gone, the builder said. I left a message on your answering machine, too.'

'I meant to get back to you, Tim, but I forgot.' While he was waiting for the right moment, he talked about the youth centre. 'We had our opening ceremony a few weeks ago. Terrific turn-out.' Once they were on their own in the sitting room, he confessed what he called his infatuation with a woman.

'I'm sure it will pass in time, but I thought I might talk it over with you.' He gave an edited version. 'A few kisses that went on too long – you know what I mean.'

Tim went through his pipe-filling ritual. 'When I was only a few years ordained, I found myself down in Wicklow. And the winter nights were long then. I remember one Christmas Eve going across to Blessington: we had run out of altar wine. The curate brought me into the kitchen where he was having his tea beside the open doors of a black range. There he was, eating kippers and brown bread, and Bing Crosby singing "White Christmas" on the wireless. Well, I sat there, keeping up the conversation and staring out of the window at the gravestones beckoning me from behind the laurel hedge.'

This was as clear a picture of clerical isolation as ever he would get. 'In those days you didn't spend much time thinking about your vocation; no such thing then as a crisis of identity.' But he knew that, unless he had some depth to his life, he would take to the bottle, or end up training the football team. 'Or maybe breeding greyhounds.'

Smoke curls rose at regular intervals. 'Celibacy will always be a sacrifice. Let's be honest: isn't it a denial of what is probably the most pleasurable experience there is?'

Brian avoided his glance.

'And if you don't believe that the sacrifice makes some sense, then all the laws in the Vatican library won't make a difference.' He motioned with an open palm towards the bookcase: ' "The strongest oaths are straw to the fire in the blood." Isn't that the way Shakespeare put it?'

'I'm nearly finished my time, but I fear for your generation.

'You're expected to be warm and friendly, and when you fall, they condemn you. If you keep your distance, you're cold and a snob. In my time, they accepted that the priest kept apart.'

'What should I do?'

'I won't tell you how you should run your life. You'll find plenty to do that. But you need some spiritual base. We live a most unusual life, and it is becoming more unusual. Unless we are convinced of that, the urge will take over. Believe me.'

Grasping at straws, Brian took up Sheridan's invitation to resume their Sunday-night walk around Dún Laoghaire. A couple of weeks later, the two men paced up and down the east pier.

Sheridan stopped and looked out across the bay. 'Did you ever hear that when a man falls in love, he may be trying to reach someone from his past?'

'How do you mean?'

'Well, I'm not an expert in these things, but one wouldn't need to be to make a few connections. You describe how this woman plays the piano: another woman in your past played the piano also.'

'So?'

'Priests are very close to their mothers, and the ould mind is a strange commodity.'

Brian tumbled to the suggestion. 'That's the best one I've heard in a long time.'

'All I'm saying is that a lot of our problems, married or celibate, come from that quarter – the past. Maybe we have to go back so that we can go forward.... Over the years I've picked up a few useful lessons from a monk down in Roscrea.'

(Mention of the monk reminded Brian of driving Sheridan to Heuston Station every June, and collecting him a fortnight later. He remembered nearing the station one time, Sheridan heaving a sigh and saying, 'The ould drink, Brian. It's a scourge.')

'No,' Brian said. 'It has nothing to do with the past. I think I know now what happened.'

They turned at the end of the pier and faced back towards Dún Laoghaire. 'I convinced myself that I was counselling a parishioner who had come with a marriage problem. Oh, I had all the jargon: "You need space to own your feelings" and such.'

'And *your* feelings?'

'Yes. My feelings in cold storage until then.'

Sheridan allowed a silence to set in before he took the next sounding. 'Did you ever think of leaving since all this happened?'

'I did.'

'And?'

He glanced at the profile sunk into the grey scarf: 'I may have come in to this chasing some vague dream, but if ever I leave, it will be in the cold light of day, I hope.'

'If you don't mind my being devil's advocate, what would you lose by leaving?'

'Well, this may sound strange from all I've told you, but I've no difficulties with the priesthood itself. I mean I could see myself in similar work if I weren't doing this. When I was in All Saints – you'll maybe laugh at this – I read *The Catcher in the Rye*, about the guy who stands at the edge of the precipice and keeps the children safe from falling over. *I* would be the catcher, Tim. In those days the sacrifice couldn't be too much. Africa – that's where I wanted to go.'

Brian stopped for a moment beside the bandstand. 'Give everything and the supreme reward awaits you: ordination, and the First Blessing to the Mother, then back home in a blaze of glory to say Mass. In a way it was like playing on the county football team, and where I come from there's no greater honour.'

'And then you find yourself counting pennies on a Monday morning.'

'Counting pennies and, when the vandals go on the rampage, taking Andy to Chadwicks so that the principal won't do the haka.'

People were coming off the ferry when the two priests returned to the car. Sheridan loosened his scarf and inserted the ignition key. 'I won't dictate to you about your life. All I'll say is, the Church needs men like you. Well, now, that walk wasn't bad.'

'It was great.' But Brian's words belied an inner fatigue. His attempt to repossess the contentment that had been his in

Beechmount failed. And some of what Sheridan had said was off the mark – what would a monk in Roscrea know about falling in love?

'Before you start up, will you give me absolution?' Brian asked.

'Of course.' Sheridan reached beneath the dashboard, unfolded a purple stole and kissed the cross before he put it around his neck. Looking out at the sea, Brian was aware of the hand raised over him in forgiveness, the little finger twisted by arthritis.

To avoid hordes of children trooping to the church the week before Christmas, he started to hear confessions from early December. He had only one class left when Brigid Mulchair rang one morning. She had seen the children from Holy Trinity going in procession and wondered if the senior classes from her school could join them. She said that Father Hegarty had told her he'd been captured by the chaplain in Brookfield House Convent to help out with the girls' confessions.

Even in Beechmount he had found children's confessions tiresome; now, to endure the sing-song list was an ordeal, and he had no intention of suffering that while Dick and Dympna window-shopped in Grafton Street and had coffee in Bewley's among the Christmas throng. He collared the other curate before he went out to say the seven-thirty Mass.

'The neurotic bitch,' Father Hegarty whispered so that the altar boy wouldn't hear. 'Didn't I tell her I'd hear them in good time? Sure we have a full week yet.' And then, as an afterthought. 'Maybe if you had an hour, we wouldn't be long getting through them. I'll ask The Ayatollah to give us a hand-out.'

The three priests waited in the sacristy for the children from Divine Grace. Before they came into view, they could hear footsteps and a murmur of voices.

'*Ciúnas*, I said. *Ciúnas!*' Miss Mulchair shrieked. 'Get into line. I am going to say it for the last time. Get into line.' Like a cockscomb, a peak of grey hair bobbed at the back as she shouted.

When the last child's confession had been heard, Brian

whipped off the violet stole and hurried down the footpath; he was gone halfway when he heard Father Brannigan call him.

'We need holly for the church. Would you ever pop up to Brookfield?' he asked in a most agreeable manner. 'Look for old Berchmans; she takes care of us every year. I'm up to my eyes and Dick says he has to visit an aunt in hospital. Good man.' The broad back disappeared inside the church before Brian had time to react.

Anyway, it was futile to protest against the directives, or the notes left through the letter box informing him of changes in the Mass roster. And he lacked the energy to argue with Brannigan; he had a heavier weight on his mind. Niamh had rung earlier. Would he go to town with her before Christmas? That was all she would ask and then she would abide by the New Year's resolution they had set — never again to meet on their own.

The thick fog that had hung in the air since morning saturated the cypresses in Brookfield; droplets clung to the weary branches and in the distance, below the sloping lawn, the naked poplars were shrouded in a grey mist.

A sparrow-like nun with gold-rimmed spectacles pulled open the heavy door, her frown dissolving when she saw the collar almost hidden by his overcoat.

'Any possibility I could see Sister Berchmans?'

'Berchmans.' The sparrow movements ceased, 'Yes, I'll get her for you, Father; you sit there and I'll get Berchmans.' In a moment, he heard the gong booming in the corridor.

Everything was in its place in the high-ceilinged parlour: the mahogany table at the centre with its enormous brass claws; over the piano the Pope looked down on him with reproving eyes. He stood to examine the hand-carved figures on the mantelpiece: mounted on a bog-oak base were facsimiles of a round tower, St Kevin's Chapel at Glendalough, and a couchant wolfhound. The inscription read: 'To Mother Mary Otteran and Community from Canon Leahy, Marian Year 1954'.

Smart footsteps approached the door; there was a knock and a much younger nun entered. She was without veil and wore the same navy habit, but on her it was more like a well-tailored uniform. 'Good Counsel tells me you're looking for Berchmans.' The smile on her delicate features was as subdued as her movements. 'I'm afraid she's not been well for the past few days. Just a head cold, and this weather doesn't help at that age.'

He explained the purpose of his visit.

'If it's only a bit of holly, I should be able to help you.' She checked the sky through the high window. 'Give me a minute to get my coat.'

At the door, Sister Good Counsel, with a loaded tray, almost collided with her. 'Now there you are,' chirped the older nun. 'Father O'Neill might like a cup of tea to warm himself and I've a cup for you too, Margaret. You probably didn't have time after school.'

While Good Counsel bustled about with cups and serviettes, Margaret caught his eye. 'You can leave the rest to me, Good Counsel. I'll look after the pouring, and thank you very much.'

She was supervising Christmas exams in the redbrick building beyond. Apart from a sabbatical in Paris, she'd been teaching in the convent school since she had qualified. 'I was at the university – Earlsfort Terrace in those days – just before the student revolt. If you can call it that.'

'We might have passed each other in the corridors then. I was there around the same time.' It was good to meet someone from a world that had almost faded from his memory. Though they had graduated in different subjects, there was a correspondence between their student days.

Forbidden to talk to lay students, they had herded together in their respective basement locker rooms for the eleven o'clock milk and currant bun, while over in the sun-drenched cafeteria of Newman House, their contemporaries flirted and made dates for Hartigans or O'Dwyer's.

She recalled old Monsignor Mulvihill, the English professor, a familiar sight in the chequered hallway, always chatting to the prettiest girls. He stopped one morning when she was waiting for the bus at Clontarf; after that he would look out for her and, as he held open the car door, she received the same roguish greeting: 'I shouldn't say this, but nothing brightens up my day as much as meeting a beautiful young woman – the world's loss and the convent's gain.'

'You know where he ended up?' Brian remarked, 'Out in the new hospital. I went to see him and he cried like a child because he had never kissed a woman – then he rambled on about Plato and the comple-mentarity of men and women.'

'Sad, isn't it, for a man who was among the top of his class in Oxford? Poor old Mull.' She settled the pleats of her skirt. 'Let's hope his dreams have been fulfilled in paradise.'

Though reluctant to leave, he returned the cup and saucer to the trolley and buttoned his overcoat. 'I suppose we'd better get going on the holly.'

She snipped the branches with the secateurs and he gathered them into a bundle. When they had finished, he drove her back to the door.

'Hold on a minute,' she said, going inside; she returned with a Christmas Cherry in a terracotta pot. 'For yourself.' She placed it on the passenger seat. 'Van Kaam and all the spiritual gurus nowadays recommend that we in religious life shouldn't neglect the senses.'

'Or else the fate of poor old Mull awaits us,' he reached across with his left hand to wish her a happy Christmas, 'and maybe some time in the New Year we'll talk about bygone days again.'

'I'll look forward to that.' She stood back and waved from the steps as he drove out of the gravelled yard.

He gave in to Niamh's pleas, and the day before Christmas Eve they met for lunch in town; she coaxed him to go to a restaurant off Grafton Street.

'One last time,' she begged. Though he knew she was drawing him back to what he wanted to forget and the places they had been together, he yielded to her wishes. At the table he glanced at the pretty face concentrated on the stiff-backed menu and winced at how close he had been to ruining both their lives. Their outrageous plans flashed across his mind: eloping to Canada and beginning a new life together. She would get a teaching job and he would return to university. Sensing his gaze, she looked up: 'Can you not take that worried look off your face. One would think all belonging to you were dead?' She rested her hand on his. 'It will be all right,' she assured him. 'Everything will be fine. This time I will make every effort to keep our resolution.'

Thirteen

The promise was broken by the third week of January. Like an addict, he found the separation unbearable. Night-times were the worst. And when he did fail, the guilt weighed on him in the morning like a hangover. Each meeting would be the last, they vowed in the afterglow of their love-making.

One evening in late spring, when the prospect of long summer days served only as a cruel reminder of his purgatory, he paced the quayside at Howth, ignoring the seagulls that swooped and screamed over the scraps brushed overboard by the fishermen. Hands buried deep in his overcoat, he cast a jaundiced eye on the cars that pulled up in front of Wright's fish shop and the women followed by children who crossed the hosed-down yard for Friday's family meal.

As darkness fell, the lights over the village traced the contours of the hill and the neon signs illuminated the shop fronts. When he moved nearer, his eye caught a huge advertisement:

'Guinness is good for you.'

He stopped. Maybe so. That night he drifted off to sleep and the following evening, he decided that a couple of pints would go well with the whiskeys he had before bedtime.

When the barman in The Kingfisher began to fill the pint as soon as he appeared inside the door, it was time to go elsewhere. He was just another man in an open-necked shirt who sat reading the evening paper or looking at the boats; nevertheless, he knew that news of his habit would travel at windspeed around Melrose if his identity were discovered. So he took other routes:

Malahide or Portmarnock, or sometimes he merged with an indifferent crowd in a city pub. There, on the high stool, he stared at the row of bottles behind the bar while all around laughed and chatted and made comments about *The Late Late Show*.

Heavy-hearted, he sat one night in the lounge of The Hillview, out beyond Clondalkin. That Friday evening, Niamh had returned his Confirmation video: she seemed to have a different excuse every week. When he backed away from her advances in the kitchen, she played her ace card: 'I'm going to London for the Whit weekend.' It was delivered in a throwaway manner and, in the silence that followed, 'I'm going on my own; I'll probably look up Harry Meegan.'

'That should be nice for you,' he'd said, despite the knot in his stomach.

'Did I ever tell you about the weekend a group of us went to Courtown?' She increased the torture, 'One night after a dance Harry took me down a lane and into a farmer's hayshed. I'd had a few drinks. If Mother had known about it, she'd have killed me.' She affected a giggle. 'Well, you know yourself the rest. We didn't go as far as they are going nowadays. But still.' She stopped and, with a distant look in her eye, chuckled as if shutting him out of a private memory.

Though he knew she wouldn't look up Meegan, he replayed the galling phrase, 'But still.' His imagination etched in the bitter details. He saw her lying on a fireside rug with Meegan of a Saturday night, heard her teasing laugh and flinched at the way she threw aside her shoes and abandoned herself to him, re-suming where they had left off many years before.

A waitress was watching him whenever she returned to the service hatch: she was pitying him and his hangdog look. When she served him, the faint smile of thanks contrasted with the self-absorbed group all around for whom she was just a facility. He had the same clean-cut looks as a teacher she had had in the vocational school. While wiping his table, even though it was the lounge-boy's job, she stole a glance: the hand that held the glass was ring-free.

'Would you care for one of these?' she asked the next time she served his drink and put beside him one of the dinner vouchers the upstairs restaurant was offering that weekend.

'Thank you.'

'And there's one for a friend.'

'A friend,' he laughed.

'Well, you never know your luck, they say.' She smiled, but winced at the glazed look in his eyes. From experience she recognized the slow movements of one who had drunk too much: was he going to drive in that state?

As the barman was closing down the steel grid over the counter, she brought him a last brandy. This time concern for his safety caused her to prolong the exchange. 'Yes, we're always busy at the weekends,' she told him. 'And by the time we're finished, the last bus is gone and I have to get a taxi.'

He looked up at her; she was wiping imaginary specks off the table. Against the haze of smoke, the Friday night commotion and the clink of glasses, he focused on her face: unless he was befuddled entirely, she was waiting for an answer.

'Maybe I could drop you off.'

She told him where she lived. 'Would it be out of your way?'

While he sat waiting for her in the car park, the effect of the drink wore off and realization of where he was dawned on him. But it was too late; she was hurrying across the tarmac, her coat on her arm. All she said was, 'Are you okay?' and then gave directions as he drove through a maze of estates until they arrived at the terraced house.

With one foot on the ground, she turned to him: 'Come and have a cup of coffee.' It was more an appeal than an invitation.

'Go on in,' she whispered in the dark hallway, indicating towards the back. 'I'll let the baby-sitter go home.'

The draining board of the kitchen sink gleamed when she put on the light; at the centre of the pine table was a basket of fruit and on the wall an earthenware plaque with an inscription: 'The more I know of human beings, the more I like my dog.'

Footsteps tripping down the stairs disturbed his inspection; when he turned round, she was at the door. The look of pity had returned. 'How do you feel?'

'I've often felt better.' He watched her nimble movements and the strain on her white blouse when she reached up for the cups.

'I'm tryin' not to be nosy, but whatever it is that's on your mind, well, I've been in the wars myself.' It was easier for her to talk while moving about. The previous Christmas Eve, her husband, after nine years of marriage, had come in and announced that he was leaving her and going to live with another woman. She pleaded with him not to abandon her, but he had made off on New Year's Day.

'Anyway I have Wayne – he's five now – and, with the job in The Hillview, I shouldn't complain.' She lit a cigarette. 'I hate the place at times. The bloke that runs the pub, you might have noticed him – he gives me the creeps. I was only a week in the place when he found out my situation and wanted to go out with me, and he has a wife and three children.' She made a face.

'I was goin' through the stocks one evening at the back when he steals up behind me. "I know how to make a fine-lookin' heifer like you happy," he says, a stupid look on his face. And by the way,' she added, 'I never do what I did tonight.'

'Bring home a stray dog.'

She smiled. 'There's something different about this stray dog and I can't make it out.'

'Let's put it like this: the stray dog is trying to forget.' He rose to his feet, but the sudden movement brought on a dizzy sensation and he had to steady himself against the table. The woman stood and reached out like someone afraid to knock over a fragile vase.

'I'm okay. Just give me a second.' A lazy grin showed on his face and he took the hand that rested against his chest. 'Ships passing in the night,' he said. 'If you don't mind, I'd prefer not to give introductions or a life history. You're a decent woman and I appreciate what you've tried to do.'

'You don't have to tell me anything,' she assured him as she drew nearer. His arm went around her waist. With his cheek nestled in her hair, he scanned the kitchen: an ironing board against the wall, a set of pots neatly housed on a rack, a child's tracksuit on a wooden clotheshorse; reminders of the woman's brave effort to overcome the rupture to her life.

But his need was too great; he shut out the reminders. He wanted to forget: forget Niamh and Melrose and lose himself with a nameless woman. A weak swimmer, he was threshing desperately to find his way to the shore.

'We'll have to be careful,' she whispered in bed when they began their love-making. The warning was superfluous. Even when she tried to arouse him, he failed to respond. And when they gave up, he lay there blinking in the darkness at the outline of the lampshade.

'It's not you,' he kept telling her, 'it's me.'

'How is that?'

'I suppose, because I know it's not right or fair. To you I mean.'

In the crook of his arm she snuggled closer. 'Don't worry, love, don't worry.' And they drifted into a fitful sleep until he woke to the cold, grey fact of where he was; the previous night was not a bad dream, her hand still lay on his chest.

She felt him looking at his watch and opened her eyes.

'I'd better get going,' he whispered and eased his arm from around her shoulder. She put a white bathrobe over her slip and on tiptoe they went out of the room.

Inside the frosted glass door, he drew her close. 'Whatever it is you are going through,' she said to his shoulder, 'I hope you are able to work out some solution.'

'Thanks.' He was about to kiss her when he became aware of activity at the top of the stairs. A little boy in his pyjamas clutching a teddy bear was looking down at them.

'Are you me Mammy's boyfriend?'

At the sound of the voice, the woman shrank from the priest's arms and swung round. For a moment she was tongue-tied; she lowered her head, one hand swept through her hair, the other clutched the neck of her bathrobe. 'Go back to bed, Wayne,' she appealed. 'I'll be up to you in a minute.'

The boy retreated. Brian and the woman stood apart, until they heard the soft footfalls overhead.

'Jesus Christ,' he raged and struck the steering wheel, 'Jee-sus

Christ, "Are you me Mammy's boyfriend".' The lost look in the waif's glazed eyes followed him all the way to Greenoaks Lawn. He turned in to his driveway. A Premier Dairies van was stopped at the top of the road, the milkman settling crates in the back while his assistant hurried up to the doors with bottles.

The stale air in the hallway surprised him, as if he had grown used to it like someone in a sickroom where only the visitor finds the smell disagreeable. His throat was dry, a sour taste rose from his stomach and he went straight to the drinks cabinet. But he stopped himself: if he started drinking in the morning, he was finished. He had a glass of water and stared out the back window, seeing only the look of wonder on the little boy peeping through the bannisters.

The clink of milk bottles on his doorstep disturbed his reflection. He waited until the van had moved off before he trudged up the stairs, thinking about his next parish duty. At eleven-thirty, he would sit in the confessional and listen to children tell how they 'spoiled love by not sharing me marbles'. Without removing shoes or clothes, he threw himself on the bed, willing sleep to his drooping spirit but knowing that guilt and despair would deny him that reprieve.

Niamh always had an excuse to keep calling; she was either looking for, or returning hymn books. But no sooner was she inside the door that the excuse went out the window and she would reveal her real agenda.

'Why do you have to keep going on about it?' she asked one evening. 'What happened between us was.only human; we can't change the way we feel.'

When the appeal failed, she lost control: 'Quite obviously you don't even want to talk to me now.'

'We've done our talking.'

'Have we now? There was plenty to talk about when you swept me upstairs. You had no talk then about vocation or priesthood.'

He could no longer control his temper. 'You weren't exactly unwilling and, as I remember it, you were the one to start the sorry mess.'

She fumbled in her handbag for a tissue. 'I was a fool ever to give myself to you. I thought you were different. You're not.' The final words she spat at him. 'You and priests like you make me sick. You go on about how lonely you are,' her face twisted with bitterness, 'as if no one else is lonely, as if thousands of married people aren't putting up with much more: half the time hating the sight of each other, or else living a lie for the sake of the children, and the neighbours.'

There was still the urge to go and sit beside her on the couch, but he knew where that would end up and he was weary of explaining that they could no longer continue as they were.

She dried her eyes. 'Tell me one thing. Was it just for sex?'

'Do you have to make it worse for both of us?'

She raised her head, her face taut with fury. 'Don't give me that nonsense. When it comes down to it, you don't care for me. When did priests ever give a fiddler's for anyone but themselves?'

He shifted in the chair. 'I'm sorry. I have to go to a meeting.'

'Oh don't let me keep you from your meeting. You've had your fun, so what would I be staying around here for? Go on to your meeting.' She reached down, picked up her shoulder bag and the hymn books and stormed out. Near the hall door she slowed her steps and turned to him, but his hand was already on the knob.

'You needn't worry,' she said. 'I'm not attempting anything. I won't bother you any more. You can go back to your Church and your priesthood and I'll try and pick up the fragments of my marriage. If it's not too late.' She paused to deliver the final blow: 'I won't embarrass you by taking Confirmation or First Communion classes next year. So you won't have to see me around.' She banged the door.

Staring at the fading image in the frosted glass, he slumped to the bottom of the stairs and blinked at the umbrella she had left behind.

He was now living for the night, when he would escape to some pub, return home after closing time and pour a large whiskey; then he would sink into the chair before the television until his head fogged with sleep. In the morning he had to fight the hangover and appear calm and even cheerful when he met the parish priest and his fellow curate, both of whom were so engrossed in their own world, they were blind to any change in him.

Seldom did he visit Paul and Orla, apart from on their wedding anniversary, the day he baptized Lisa, their first born, or a bank holiday weekend; anyway, Paul was busy with his studies. That autumn he would receive his Masters in psychology and the professor was urging him to continue his research for a doctorate. Already a financial corporation was employing him on a temporary basis.

One Sunday in early June, they invited him over for the day. It was too fine to stay indoors, so after lunch they sat out in the back garden; Brian and Orla on the two deckchairs facing the sun, Paul in the shadow of the high surrounding wall. Beside him Lisa lay on the rug.

'Is it my imagination or have you put on weight, Brian?' Orla asked as she looked over the batch of christening photographs.

Paul interrupted his play with Lisa: 'You know these priests, love, they never do an honest day's work.'

Brian laughed it off and felt for a gathering of flesh at the waist of his shirt. 'Middle-age spread, Orla.'

On the way home he sank beneath another brooding cloud: life was passing him by. Most of his year from St Bernard's had wives and children on the brink of adolescence: the last school reunion had brought that home to him. The following October, Donal's eldest would begin her university studies in Cork. And Orla and Paul were so self-absorbed, they were blind to his pain. It would be a long time before they would have a visit from him again.

When the summer holidays came round, life once more deserted the grounds of Holy Trinity School, where the main gate was a meeting place for parents at midday. The playground too was silent, apart from the few who hit tennis balls during the Wimbledon fortnight. Fewer came to the Sunday Mass, some had mobile homes and disappeared to Rush and Donabate for the weekend. Only those with Mass cards and government forms requiring a signature called to his house.

The solitude was a mixed blessing. He didn't have to visit the classrooms, or make a show of interest in the children's artwork, priests like snowmen with raised arms saying Mass. In addition, he was saved from the pain of meeting Niamh in the corridor and seeing the face he had once kissed, now white-hot with resentment. Occasionally, while in the school to pay the cleaners, he stopped at the open door of her room and looked around at the chairs standing on the desks. The sprig of heather set in glass, his present from Connemara, was still on the wall. He made perfunctory visits to the youth centre to ensure that the leaders were following the programme, but could endure the din for a short while only.

On the way back one evening, he passed by the forecourt of Davis Towers where a couple of girls were playing with a child. When they saw him, they hurried with the toddler to the palisade fence.

'Hello, Father O'Neill,' they chorused.

'Hello, girls.'

'Father O'Neill, you don't come into our class like you done last year.'

'I was very busy before the holidays, girls, but I'll start again in September.'

'An' Father O'Neill,' another chirped up, 'Missus Kirwan told us about Judas.' She was nearly breathless. 'Judas was a bad man, even though Jesus loved him. An' he went up an' kissed him an' Jesus said "Judas, are you goin' to betray me." Was he a bad man, Father?'

'We should never say that about anyone, because we never know the full story.' He tried to explain, but the child's soother fell on the concrete and he began to bawl until they bent down to fuss over him.

The chaplain in Brookfield went on supply to a parish outside Boston, and priests from the locality were asked to say the convent Mass. Tuesday and Friday were assigned to Melrose.

'The Superior up there asked The Ayatollah and he volunteered the two of us,' Dick told Brian. 'You can be sure he won't move his fat arse out of bed at that hour – we'll pay for his free lunches in the convent.'

Dick was supposed to take the Tuesday morning Mass, but invariably he phoned Brian on the Monday night. Would he do a big favour and say the Mass in the morning? The story varied: he had to see someone off at the airport, or else one of his ordination class was having a party and it would go on until the small hours.

Often hungover, Brian found it an ordeal to rise so early and compose himself, but after a while he was drawn to the protected world inside the high gates: a haven from the chaos that ravaged his soul. He broke his habit of going out to drink and settled for a large whiskey on the nights before he said early Mass. While he vested in the sacristy, the nuns sang Matins, their choral chant pouring consolation on his inner commotion. After Mass, until the peace was shattered by the arrival of Spanish students, he wandered around the grounds.

In front of the main door, flowerbeds formed a Celtic cross design before the lawn sloped down to the river. Between the row of beeches was a vista of the Dublin mountains.

Sister Margaret returned after two weeks with her family in Wexford. She looked in one morning when he was finishing his breakfast. 'You look as though you need a holiday yourself.' She gave him a searching glance but he parried the remark and reverted to the account of her holiday, the shopping trips to New Ross with her sister-in-law.

Later, she steered the conversation back to Melrose: 'It can't be easy in a parish these days with such growing indifference.' With a gossamer touch, her fingers smoothed the tablecloth. He grew tense: 'Can't do much about that now, Margaret.' He shrugged. 'The dole queue is too long and as the steward in the gospel put it, "To dig I am unable, to beg I am ashamed."'

She wasn't put off. 'It can be difficult here too. The days I fear most are the holidays when everyone disappears, off to get books from the library or to visit relatives, and the whole house is empty, except for someone down in the basement doing her ironing.'

He saw where it was leading: an invitation to remove the mask. Her womanly intuition had seen through the act and he was tempted to unload the burden. She would understand. But he held out, muttering agreement about the difficulties of religious life; then he wiped his mouth with the napkin and folded it in the silver ring. 'I'm afraid I'll have to be going, Margaret.' Rising from the table, he caught the silent regret in her face.

A few evenings later, he was seated inside the window of his front room, trying to concentrate on the breviary he held on his crossed knee. Every so often a football game in progress at the back of the church intruded into his prayer. He placed the ribbon marker between the pages, went inside to the drinks cabinet and returned with a glass and a bottle of Crested Ten. A shout went up that caused him to raise his head: the goalkeeper was gathering the ball from the net and pointing recriminations at his defenders. Another season was beginning for the soccer players – the first sign of the slow turning point towards autumn.

Evenings in Danagher's Field with the Gaelic team floated into his mind: the sheer delight in springing off the ground, soaring higher than the others and plucking the ball from out-reaching fingers. Then the momentary search for the player running loose along the wing and the well-aimed kick that reached its target, bringing yells of excitement from the men in caps and sunburnt faces who stood along the sideline. The same men had decorated the village with banners, and the football team formed a guard of honour up the steps of the church when he had returned to say his first Mass. He had been the first player from the parish since 1952 to receive the county jersey, but had to forgo the honour when he entered All Saints.

He took the bottle off the table, trudged to the sitting room and sank into the chair. He reached for the remote control and flicked from one channel to another and back again.

The sound of the door bell activated a panic button in his brain; of late the phone would have the same effect. He sprang up, hid the bottle and glass and rushed for the packet of mints he kept behind the clock. Then he picked up a pen and ambled to the door.

'Margaret.' For a moment he was speechless, and then overdid the welcome. 'It's great to see you. Come in, come in, Margaret.'

He took refuge making coffee and small talk through the open door of the kitchen, hoping that no trace of his drinking remained in the sitting room. She had convent news: who was away on holidays, who was going on the missions and who was moving to another post.

'And you?' She came to the door and rested against the frame, her arms folded beneath the cardigan draped around her shoulders. 'What are you doing for the holidays, or is that information strictly private?'

'A bit like your situation: two weeks at home – race week in Tralee and then a few days to relax.' He handed her a cup of coffee. 'I used to go to America when I taught in the Tech, or spend a couple of weeks in France with Paul Duggan. Now it has to be Banna Strand in September.'

'You'll have the place to yourself at that time.'

'Yes. Lonely Banna Strand. It's the name of a song, you know.'

'I suppose you get used to it.'

About to say 'Yes, you do', he choked on the words. Suddenly his breezy manner was engulfed in an unbearable fit of sadness, like a mourner who meets an old friend at a graveside. His words were slow and deliberate and sounded strange to his own ears: 'No. You don't get used to it. No, you don't. And I don't know how much longer I can put up with this.' Like the onrush of a flood, the force of his words cracked the barrier of his resistance and the wall came tumbling down. The fear and guilt and pain came out in a convulsive fit of weeping. He no longer cared about control, or shame, and the torrent of feelings he had strangled for months gushed forth.

Margaret reacted instinctively. In a swift movement that caused her cardigan to fall on the carpet, she was kneeling beside him, her hand on his arm.

'One thing after another,' he moaned. 'How much is a fellow supposed to take for God's sake?'

'Don't bottle it up,' she kept repeating. 'It's better to talk.'

'First they shift you from one place to another, then you find yourself with a fellow whose only interest is writing stupid histories of the glory days because he can't face what's happening. Then Paul goes; and others – and what's left?' He blurted out about himself and Niamh Kirwan, and even though he knew it was well and truly over, guilt from the episode filled him with misery. Last of all he told her of his drinking habits.

After a long silence, he raised his head. 'Well, now you know and you're the only one who knows. A good friend of mine, Tim Sheridan, knows some of what I've told you. I just couldn't tell him the full story. Do I get absolution?'

'I'll have to think up a penance first.' She sat on a chair nearby. 'Do you think you may be hooked on the drink?'

'I haven't seen any elephants climbing up walls, if that's what you mean. No, I'd say it's only a question of breaking a habit.'

'Or maybe absolving yourself. Do you think you can do that or will you keep reproaching yourself for the rest of your life?'

Exhausted, he relaxed into the chair.

The nun's visit that evening was not the coincidence she had intimated at the door; however, this was not the time, she judged, to give an explanation. She had stumbled on the truth of his drinking: a chance meeting with a cleaning woman had revealed the reason for his tired look.

The cleaner had rested the can of Mr Sheen on the window ledge and kept polishing the wooden panel. She boasted to Margaret that she was now a collector of the church envelopes in Davis Towers, though few had subscribed since the trouble in Divine Grace School. The creases in her weather-beaten face deepened; she squeezed her mouth into a smile: 'Father Brannigan asked me. A lovely man. We have lovely priests in our parish. Great priests. God bless them. And the new man.' She chuckled. 'I still call him the new man, Sister. He was in me house one evenin' doin' his rounds. Sure, he's no more than a chap.'

She lowered her voice. 'Fond of his drink, he is, Sister Margaret.' She stopped polishing, 'Come here till I tell you. Our Tracy works in the check-out over in Coolock where he does his shoppin' and every week he has a couple of bottles from the drinks counter.'

The woman with the hatchet face was so engrossed in her story, she was unaware of the nun's changed expression. 'I wouldn't tell that to anyone only yourself.' She was now whispering, because the Sisters were going to the refectory for afternoon tea. 'And someone saw him a few nights in The Kingfisher.'

'Let's go in here for a moment, Mrs Judge.' Margaret had ushered her towards the linen room and closed the door.

'You see, Mrs Judge, what we don't often realize is that priests have to entertain parishioners and Father O'Neill is probably a generous man and gives a drink to the men who count the money on Monday nights. I know priests who do that.' The hint of disapproval was not lost on Mrs Judge.

'Yes,' she said and aimlessly began to run a cloth along the top of a shelf. 'Of course, and they're great priests. God bless them, and I wouldn't tell that to anyone but yourself, Sister Margaret.'

For Brian, the blessed relief of telling everything fused with those moments when he had emerged from the dark confessional in St Bernard's. He was cleansed of the dreaded mortal sins: nights in the wooden cubicle when he feasted his imagination on a glimpse of a stocking-top he had spied that day when a woman was working the pedals of her bicycle on College Street, or on Gina Lollobrigida in *Come September*, when it was shown in the Astor during the Easter holidays.

By the time he had finished his story, darkness was falling outside. He got up. 'Now,' he said, 'to prove my sincere purpose of amendment, witness this.' He took the bottle of whiskey and glass from behind his chair, and directed her to follow him to the kitchen where he unscrewed the cap and emptied the contents down the sink. He held the bottle until the gurgle from the drainpipe subsided; the smell of whiskey rose from the sink and he turned on the cold tap and left it running.

' "Oh wash me whiter than snow," ' he quoted, almost to himself.

'You'll be okay,' she reassured his hunched shoulders; her hand lightly brushed his back. After a moment the brushing ground to a halt. 'I don't believe it.'

'You don't believe what?' He turned round to see a look of surprise mingled with amusement on her face; she was gazing out at the back garden, where thistles rubbed against the window and puffball spores loosened and floated in the breeze. Above the rank grass, yellow stalks of ragwort and dockweed dotted the swaying jungle. He tried to shrug it off. 'It reflects the state of my soul.'

The condition of the garden led her to a discreet inspection of the kitchen. 'I know,' he said, reading her thoughts; 'it needs a good cleaning. I had a woman coming in a couple of times a week, but I let her go – afraid she might discover something. You know how they talk.'

'I do indeed.... Look, you can tell me it's none of my business, but if you like I could come over tomorrow and help you with a spring clean.'

'That's decent of you.' He thought for a moment. 'And maybe I'll get out and attempt something with this forest.'

He was pouring petrol into the lawnmower when she pulled up in the blue Renault the following morning. She waved, removed her sunglasses and put them in the case beneath the dashboard. After a cup of coffee, they set to work and continued until well after midday. The growth was so advanced that he had to lean on the handles of the lawnmower so that the front was raised; even then, rank grass and weeds clogged up the blade and often the engine cut out. As he raked up the garden, the rich smell of grass and the juices of severed stalks rose from the moist earth.

He cast off his tennis shoes, now coated in green, and, on his way upstairs, thrust his head inside the dining-room door. She was polishing the table.

'Van Kaam,' he grinned, and nodded towards the vase of flowers on the piano. The room looked bright, the air was fresh; the leaded glass on the bookcase sparkled.

'The labourer is worthy of her hire,' he said. 'And if you don't have other commitments, I'd like to treat you to lunch.'

'That's a fair wage.'

The midday rush had subsided in the Saint Lawrence Hotel, so they were given one of the tables that fitted into the embrasure of a bay window, where they could look out at the boats lazing in the harbour. 'It was a strange feeling when I woke this morning,' he remarked after they had ordered. 'The first reaction was the one I've lived with for some time now – I've to face another so-and-so day; cover the head and hide. As if one could find such a place.'

'And now?'

'Now. Well, I'm not so foolish as to think that my troubles are over, but you'll never know how much your visit helped me.'

She straightened herself so that the waitress could place the two bowls of soup on their table.

Fourteen

He resumed his rounds of golf with Lynsky and Looby. The first Thursday in Portmarnock was as stale as all the others; Looby even retold some of his sex jokes.

A major question perplexed the mind of every priest on the golf course that day: who would be the next archbishop? They had been waiting over a year for a successor to Archbishop Downey, who had died suddenly in Italy. In that time, rumours of likely successors abounded, one following on the heels of another.

Looby had a full account of those who were seeking favour with Rome. Monsignor Somers, his parish priest, had dined in the Nunciature the previous week. 'That's where the power is, lads. The Nuncio claims that his man always is acceptable to Rome.' The tinny laugh rang out over the golf course. 'Of course he was wined and dined, and your man played for them afterwards.'

The Nuncio's recitals on the cello were well-known: fawning clerics sat around, glasses of Galiano in hand, and outdid each other in praising his virtuosity.

'Somers is pushing Eddie Shorthall. It seems that the Maynooth man hasn't a pup's chance: too soft on the divorce issue.'

'Wouldn't he be a breath of fresh air?' Brian suggested.

'They've had enough fresh air since the Vatican Council.'

Father Shorthall appeared frequently in the newspapers. He

expressed concern about the fabric and sanctity of family life, and deplored the number of young girls who were giving birth to children out of wedlock. At the finals in Croke Park, he sat behind the cardinal, and when the captains came to receive the trophy, he clapped vigorously. The cunning looks, however, showed through his laughing mask.

Senior priests saw Shorthall as an excellent choice. 'Hadn't he got first place in Canon law?' And if he met them in Wynn's or outside McCaul's, the clerical outfitters, he always remembered their names.

After months of rumours and talk of deputations to the Papal Nuncio, the announcement came suddenly. Brian was having his lunch when the one o'clock news reported that the new archbishop was Raymond Gilmore. The previous year, the religious correspondent said, Gilmore had been released from his teaching duties to work in the Vatican. Recently he had received commendation from Rome for a series of articles defending the Pope's refusal to grant laicization to priests: the series was entitled 'His Hand to the Plough.'

Father Brannigan was delighted with the announcement.

'Ray is a fine man. An excellent choice. He was a year ahead of me in the Gregorian. Great brain you know.'

Dick Hegarty nodded solemnly. 'He'll keep the liberals in their place. Did you see the way he dealt with that witch on the telly when she brought up about married priests? As if we didn't have enough problems without having to look after a wife as well. Am I right, Leo?'

All the priests of the diocese received invitations to the installation in the Pro-Cathedral on the last Sunday in April. But Brian had a gilt-edged excuse for not attending: it was his turn to officiate at baptisms. Anyway, he had seen it all before when the archbishop had been installed. After the ceremony, All Saints would swarm with priests for the reception. And all the initial objections, 'He is totally unsuited – no experience of parish work,' or 'He has a fishy handshake,' would be washed away in the high tide of celebration.

That Sunday evening, Brian drove over to Brookfield and waited in the convent parlour for Sister Margaret.

'You must be the only priest in Dublin not in the Pro-Cathedral today,' was her greeting as she crossed the room to where he stood looking out of the high window.

'I've been there before.'

'The less liberated of us and the elderly were glued to the set all afternoon, but the feminists refused to watch what they called a show of clerical power.'

'Insubordinate wretches,' he grinned. 'God be with the days when a little nun's greatest ambition was to serve the monsignor's rasher and egg, and listen like a mouse to his list of achievements.'

She laughed.

The fine evening drew them down to the river and along the embankment until the red-brick building was out of sight.

'So why didn't you go to the ordination?' she asked.

'I was on baptisms.'

'And the real reason?'

'The shenanigans that went on for the past couple of months. Did I tell you? We were within an ace of getting Eddie Shorthall until three seminary professors, one from All Saints, went to Armagh to protest. Seems the cardinal was unhappy about Shorthall, so he went over the Nuncio's head and flew to Rome. Gilmore was a compromise.'

'So much for the Holy Spirit.'

'I'm afraid the Holy Spirit wouldn't have much room in that company.'

'Does it bother you?'

'Not much. I think I've come to accept that's the way life is, inside or outside the Church.' He shrugged. 'Maybe I've learned a bit more about myself also. I took things too seriously. The zealous young priest – you know what I mean – available at all hours. I was the one who would bring back the lost sheep. Convert everything that moved.'

Across the river, windows of houses were squares of burnished copper in the setting sun. 'Anyway, Margaret, I went straight from one boarding-school to another.'

'Had you much experience of life, I mean, had you ever gone with girls before you went into All Saints?'

'If you consider a few harmless cuddles with Teresa Lawlor the year we did our Leaving, then I went with a girl. The nearest I got to a last fling was during a Rose of Tralee week.'

The details were fresh in his mind. On stage at the Ashe Ballroom, Butch Moore and the Capitol Showband, then at their peak, were delighting the swaying crowd. Before the dance was over, he left with Teresa and strolled through the town park. Music, the voice of the ringmaster and bursts of applause rose from the circus tent. Fireworks shot up into the clear sky as they walked towards the town, where some wizard had transformed the streets with necklaces of coloured lights. From above the throb of the milling crowd came screams of excitement from the swinging-boats and the Ferris wheel.

'She knew by then that I was headed for All Saints the following week. It didn't stop us, though, from having a good old court against the monastery wall.'

They rested for a while on the narrow bridge near the end of the walk and watched the cattle grazing; a rusted horse rake lay against the hedge, the wooden shaft moss-green.

'There's a similarity between our stories.' She sniffed at a buttercup.

'How?'

'The way we didn't have time to consider other possibilities.'

'Did you not have time?'

'No. Having two aunts in the congregation more or less sealed my fate.'

Sister Victoire and Sister Malachy wrote constantly to their niece; they enclosed booklets about the saints' lives: 'The Little Flower', 'Maria Goretti' or the life of their foundress. When Margaret was thirteen, the aunts, along with her mother, put their heads together, and decided that she should attend the boarding-school where Sister Victoire was Mother Superior. It was no surprise to the others when she was made Head Girl in her final year: up until then she had been a Child of Mary, and president of the Pioneer Total Abstinence Association. Invariably she was the one chosen to deliver the address of welcome to distinguished guests like Kenneth Kaunda, the first President of Zambia.

The family visited a couple of times during the term. The initial strangeness in the parlour between Margaret and her younger siblings soon wore off when she warmed to their backlog of news from home.

In fine weather, they sauntered around the walled garden, her mother walking in front with her aunt and she alongside her father, the same manly smell of pipe tobacco emanating from his loose tweeds. Some days he sat in the green Vauxhall and read the Sunday papers, the door open and one cherry brown shoe resting on the tarmac.

On one of these Sundays, while the children were playing around the pond, fragments of whispered confidences reached Margaret's ears. It was a sultry day, but the bitter tone was chilling. 'They're all the same. Men. Only out for what they can get.' Her mother's look of disdain towards the Vauxhall shattered her. For the first time, the significance of father and mother in separate beds sank like lead to the pit of her stomach.

Fifteen

Though he sometimes slid back into ruts of self-doubt, Brian found within himself a slow change that was akin to recovery after illness. Mental fatigue and hangovers, for long his morning adversaries, had now disappeared and he was able to settle down to his parish duties, relieved of the compulsion that had driven him to run from himself. Even at low ebb, he had never failed to turn up, nor had he asked his next door neighbour to cover for him.

At times he envied the domestic fortress Dick Hegarty had created, Dympna hanging out his washing, the two of them behind the trolley at the supermarket, and the fable that evoked admiration from the parishioners: 'Isn't Father Hegarty great the way he looks after his cousin since her husband died?'

Sometimes, Paul's preoccupation with his family, his work and their new house raised objections in his mind to what he had taken for granted in the past about friendship and loyalty between priests. But he nodded to the grown-up voice within: yes, of course, Paul had to do what was right. That assent, however, failed to staunch the trickle of resentment that seeped through the self-evident truth.

And for all his preaching about love, unity and intimacy, he wondered, in dark moments, if anyone cared a straw about him. Even Margaret, who had lifted him out of the pit, left him in no doubt about what mattered most in her life.

In a few years his mother would be gone. That brutal truth had hit him the last time he was down in Kerry, when he heard her shuffling to the fridge; such a short time before, she had been so light on her feet when she prepared dinner for the whole family on St Stephen's Day.

But he had gained an insight that had changed his life – no longer would he crowd his days with work, as he had done in Beechmount. He was a man before he was a priest. In a painful way, Niamh Kirwan had taught him a lesson; at least, she had taught him the need for a woman's company, not just for his priesthood, but to save him from going mad.

When he returned one evening after a game of golf, his eye fell on a note caught in the letter box: he recognized the parish priest's handwriting as he set the bag of clubs beneath the stairs. It was a summons to a meeting the following day.

Shirt-sleeves folded to the elbow, Brannigan was attaching strips of print to a board when Brian arrived for the meeting. 'This is for the church porch. I'll explain it all when Dick turns up – if he does.' The parish priest offered him a glimpse of his handiwork.

In boldfaced print the poster announced a parish social in the Crofton Hotel; proceeds would go towards the setting-up of a parish social service centre. When Dick joined them, the parish priest briefed his curates on the strategy for success. 'I want you two chaps,' he cocked his forefingers like pistols, 'to get cracking on the sale of tickets through the schools. Leave no stone unturned.' He reached down and picked up two bundles of leaflets. 'And you can start by giving around these flyers.'

Dick read the leaflet: 'Well done, Leo.'

Brian studied his copy. 'You have down here,' he said to Brannigan without raising his head, 'the twenty-eighth of May. Isn't that the night before the First Communions in Divine Grace?'

Dick took out his diary and turned the pages. 'I'm afraid Brian is right.'

An awkward silence followed. The parish priest's bushy eyebrows knitted, the ruddy complexion deepened and he studied the clipboard as if it held some solution to the conundrum.

Eventually, he raised his head, but the eyes remained fixed on the board: 'That won't make any difference. No, I don't foresee any difficulty. I want to explain to you about the parish social service I'm setting up. I can rely on your backing. That social worker bitch, Harding, is up to her tricks again.' He scratched his head. 'I believe she's advising silly women to walk out on their husbands if they say a cross word to them. I've known for a long time that she's been telling them to go on the Pill.'

'She's a right bitch, Leo,' said Dick.

'Well, we're going to have our own counselling service, and we have to raise funds to get it off the ground. The Catholic Marriage Union is willing to row in with us on this. We have to preserve the sanctity of the family. And uphold the Pope's encyclical.'

'Good man yourself: you were right to put it up to Leo,' Dick said as soon as they had left the parish priest and his clipboard. 'I was going to challenge him myself anyway. He's more set on getting the better of Harding than the children's Holy Communion. Leo is in a sulk because the people are going to her with their problems rather than coming to us. She has a line of people outside her office every Monday. We're left with the likes of Mary Ann Cummiskey and a few children on Saturday night.'

Over the low wall, he called, 'Drop in tonight if you're free. We'll chew the fat.'

Except for the occasional visit, such as the FA Cup final or a major golf tournament, when they had a couple of drinks together before the television, the two priests kept to themselves. The only trace of Dympna the junior curate ever saw on those visits was a pair of high heels thrown under the sideboard or a cardigan draped over the back of an armchair.

'It's all a power game.' Dick placed the whiskey bottle and the mixers on the glass-protected mahogany table and resumed where he had left off earlier. 'I've seen his crowd in action and they're all the same. Frustrated men. They need to bully. That writer, what's his name? *The Shoes of the Fisherman*.'

'Morris West.'

'He was right: "Power is the lust of the celibate." And now they're scared because they know the Church is losing ground. The glory days are gone.'

'They're probably very unhappy.'

'In some ways they're happier than you or me. Leo has his golf on a Wednesday and his game of cards out in Muredach's on Sunday night. But they're short on human feeling. Dead from the neck down.' He laughed at his own quip.

As the whiskey took effect, he mellowed and stretched back on the recliner: 'Ah, sure, I suppose, Brian, we're all more to be pitied than blamed, including Leo. Eunuchs for the kingdom,' he chortled. 'Fecking eunuchs.' He filled their glasses again.

'Now do you know what I'm going to tell you and maybe I've a bit more experience of these things.' He tapped the arm rest. 'Any priest needs company; otherwise, you'd go off your nut or else become like Leo – bossing poor old Sister Fidelis around or trying to get the upper hand of Harding.' The dancing blue eyes took the measure of the other man's reaction. 'Oh I don't mean you do anything wrong; just a bit of company around the place.'

He chuckled and sank back into the armchair, nursing the whiskey as if it were a precious vessel. 'You know, you're a bit of a mystery to me. You're so independent. I admire the way you stand up to that arsehole.'

Brian was tempted to dispel the wrong impression and let him know how close he had moved to the edge, but he resisted. He had no intention of having his personal life whispered about at Royal Dublin the following week.

He twirled his whiskey glass. 'About the independence bit. You're long enough on the road to know that you never judge the book by its cover.'

'I suppose you're right.' The remark brought on another senseless chuckle and he reached for the bottle. He was about to refill his confrère's glass but Brian covered the rim with his hand. 'Thanks, Dick, but I'd have a splitting headache if I drank any more.'

The bottle still hovered over the covered glass until Dick knew he meant it. 'I don't know what's wrong with these young fellows nowadays,' he asked himself, and in the act of stretching broke wind. 'Sorry,' he laughed, 'Ah, well, better out than in, what? Anyway, good luck.' Both priests raised their glasses.

The First Communion Mass over, Dick responded to the custo-
mary call to stand with each child for the photograph; after a
while, Brian returned to tidy up the sacristy. Putting away the
cruets and the vestments, he could hear the tinkle of coins and
Father Brannigan humming next door. He smiled.

Like a small boy who wakes early to play with a new toy, the
parish priest had gone straight to the office as soon as he had
helped with the distribution of Communion. Every now and
again the humming was interrupted to check figures with Sister
Fidelis.

The buoyant mood continued over the weekend. On
Monday he invited the two curates to a meal in the Skylon.

'A credit to you, Leo.' No sooner were they seated at the table
than Dick rejoiced in the honeymoon atmosphere.

'What was the final count?'

'We haven't got in the last of the ticket money, but already
we're a thousand pounds ahead of what we predicted.' From the
top pocket of his shirt he produced a lodgement slip and took
another look before he handed it to the curates. 'There's a
breakdown.'

Hegarty whistled in disbelief. 'That's massive, Leo.' Parish
business was forgotten and the conversation evoked memories
of bazaars and other events. Brannigan recalled better days when
he was a curate in Skerries and the parish priest and himself got
the farmers' wives to bake and collect produce for the Christmas
fairs, summer sports and dances. One time they even wrangled a
three-year-old bull for the raffle from a local cattle dealer.

As soon as he arrived back at the house, Brian checked the
answering machine. Muredach Hogan had a message from the
cleaners, who wanted their money early because of the bank
holiday weekend; Looby reminded him about Thursday in Royal
Dublin Golf Club.

The three priests were earlier than usual at the golf club that
week because Lynsky had an appointment with the archbishop
at five o'clock. Dewdrops still twinkled in the grass and the
foghorn boomed out in Dublin Bay as they prepared to tee off.

Before long, however, the veil of mist that hung over Howth melted into the blue sky, and by noon-time a couple of men who had forgotten to bring caps knotted handkerchiefs over their shining crowns. Lynsky was eager to impart the importance of his meeting; he dropped a few hints, but the others were too concentrated on their strokes to notice. Finally he edged in his unasked-for news.

'I got the fright of my life,' he told them, 'when I got a call from headquarters that the boss wanted to see me. My first reaction was that they needed some statistics on the marriage scene. I've been working on that for a few months.' He fixed his gaze on the hill. 'Then over a cup of coffee, His Nibs makes his announcement. "I want you to go to Rome for a year to pursue further studies on marriage and the family." I nearly dropped the cup.' His Nibs asked him to think about it for two weeks and to return on the Thursday. 'Swotting in the heat of Rome is not exactly my ideal way of spending the summer. Then I'm supposed to have a working lunch once a week with Monsignor Franzoni, the cardinal's right-hand man.'

'God help you,' Looby made easy the inevitable assent. 'You've no choice when His Nibs calls.'

'Ah, well,' said Lynsky with a few practice swings at the final tee, 'anything for Mother Church.'

The mannered submission was transparent to the others; they knew Lynsky was aiming high. At clerical gatherings such as the diocesan retreat, he strolled the grounds with Iggy Somers, or one of the other monsignors who were known to have influence. 'Lynsky may joke and fool around with Looby, but make no mistake about it, he has his own agenda.' Paul's comment came winging back to Brian as he watched the Rome-bound priest whack the ball down the fairway.

They had a glass of beer and a sandwich afterwards in the bar; then with a tap on the car roof, Brian left them: 'Good luck with the meeting, Philip.'

'Thanks. See you next Thursday.'

'See you, Brian.' Looby leaned over, and the tyres crunched loose pebbles on the tarmac.

Like others who had been faithful to that pattern since ordination, the two priests would return later for dinner at the club. The table-talk inevitably veered towards which priests were near to retirement. They shared every morsel: who had been passed over for promotion, or who was giving trouble to his parish priest. And every year younger men joined the group and fitted into the mould with the unerring instinct of homing pigeons.

Brian had time to spare before the evening Mass, so he drove on past the turn-off point until he reached Dollymount Strand. Away towards the city, the sea sparkled like ripped silver paper, and through a break in the cloud, rays of sun beamed on the Pigeon House. His excuse about the seven-thirty Mass freed him from attending the club dinner, but also left him with nothing to do on such a glorious evening. He was tempted to visit Brookfield but knew that the unspoken boundaries Margaret had established precluded frequent meetings.

Soon she would be off for most of the summer to the congregation's convent outside Paris. The argument they had had over that still chafed. 'What's wrong with my visiting Paris for a week? I'd stay at the Irish College; we could have a few great days.'

Whenever her mind was made up, such an appeal fell on deaf ears.

'Leaving aside the fact that I cannot do that, much as I would like to; surely you can guess how that would be grist to the mill for the gossipers.'

'I don't care about the gossipers,' and seeing that he was fighting a lost cause, he delivered a lecture on 'nuns who take shelter behind high walls because they can't face the world.'

Later when he recalled the look of hurt on her pale face, he was filled with self-loathing and a Waterstone's book-token was offered sheepishly as atonement.

He was learning that the growing desire he had towards her must be curbed; she was affectionate, but the limits were unmistakeable. If, while embracing, she sensed his arousal or indeed an incipient response from herself, she withdrew immediately. In the aftermath of these frustrations he regretted that he had become a priest and wished he was free to satisfy what he had begun to see as healthy, natural desires.

He was no sooner in from the seven-thirty Mass than the phone rang; he grabbed the receiver before the answering machine went into action. The sound of her voice set him on edge; yet he spoke calmly. 'Niamh. It's great to hear from you.'

'Liar,' she said and laughed. 'Don't worry. It isn't a relapse. If you have an hour, I'd like to see you tomorrow. We've the day off.'

'Sure.' Threads of the old anxiety wormed their way through him. 'Call after Mass.'

'I was thinking of later. Lunch?'

He hesitated.

'Trust me.'

'All right.'

To occupy his mind before she arrived, he applied himself to work he had avoided until the last minute: sorting out circulars from the Department of Education, filling in forms for teachers who had applied for career breaks, and making out the agenda for the next board of management meeting.

The tap of her heels on the driveway and the familiar clearing of her throat caused something inside him to tighten. He was at the door almost as soon as she rang the bell. Everything about her – the perfect figure in the navy dress with a row of white buttons down the front, the scent of her perfume – threatened once more to entangle him in the net from which he had escaped. He led her to the front room and, after a moment of unease, when words seemed to desert both of them, he turned out to the hallway.

'I'll only be a minute.' He took a leather jacket from the coat hanger. When he returned, she was looking around the room; her inspection stopped at the davenport desk.

'That's beautiful.' She ran nail-polished fingers up and down the green leather slab.

'I picked it up in an auction room.' Fragments of the day he and Margaret had strolled along the quays came back to him. He looked at his watch. 'I booked for one o'clock, so we'd better get going.'

She seemed reluctant to leave: 'I'd hardly know the place: you've been doing some decorating. Lovely.'

As if conditioned by a ritual, she drove off in her car and he waited for about ten minutes to scatter any suspicion in his next door neighbour: the same as when they had been meeting secretly.

In the restaurant, he glanced at her while she read the menu. She showed no trace of the gloom that had weighed on their troubled meetings. Instead, he saw the sparkle of that first day in her classroom.

'Incidentally,' she reassured him, without raising her head, 'you needn't worry any more. I'm over it now; well, over the madness anyway. I know I acted the bitch at times, but you understand, don't you, that I'd lost all sense? I'd have done anything to hold on to you.' She looked up. 'If you hadn't been so strong in the end, God knows what harm we'd have done to each other. And that was one reason I asked you out today.'

'And the other?'

'Shane has finally agreed to come with me to a counsellor.'

'I'm glad. Really glad for you.' He meant it. And yet from some crevice of his mind seeped a trickle of loss at the finality of it all.

'I'm not going overboard about it. He had to see a cardiologist a few months ago, who told him that if he didn't alter his lifestyle, he'd be playing a harp in the clouds for his fiftieth birthday.'

On the way back they stopped at the car park in Sandymount and walked along by the shore.

'It's a relief that it has worked out all right,' he said, more confident now that she seemed at peace.

They stood, looking towards Dún Laoghaire and beyond where clouds blurred the outline of the hills.

'I learned a costly lesson,' she said. 'In a way I was waiting for you, or someone like you. But I know now we would have been a disaster together. You will think this is cracked. You know that song you used to play on the piano about being put on a pedestal.'

'The Ann Murray one. "You Needed Me".'

'That's it. And that's exactly what I felt: as if you had put me on a pedestal.'

At length, he asked the question that was pressing for an answer. 'Do you think it did any harm, I mean, how are things since?'

'No better or no worse than many couples; a lot better than those who go on about how great their husbands are. I hear them when I'm beneath the dryer or at the tennis club. I know well that most of it is pretence.' She paused, 'You learn to cut your losses, and get on with life.'

'One of the teachers boasts in the staff room that her husband never forgets to get Interflora to deliver a bouquet to the house, if they've had a row the evening before. Bilge. You should hear the talk when she's not there, about the way he flirts with the girls in the office.'

They both laughed and a flicker of the old excitement passed between them.

Farther out, a boy was throwing a stick into the shallow water for a dog to bound after it; lazy plumes of smoke rose from a chimney of the Pigeon House. The silence between them no longer threatened. They were two climbers resting on a mountain-top after a punishing ascent.

He was about to switch on the ignition when she laid a hand on his forearm. 'I know I said awful things and how you took it all, God only knows, but I needed reconciliation. Come in to the classroom sometime if you want to. But I will understand if you can't.'

'And now,' a blush rose to her cheeks, 'start the car.'

On the way home the girls came first in her thoughts. Sonya had done her Masters in Economics and was hoping to go to London for work experience, though Shane wanted her to join his firm. Andrea's eating disorder seemed to be under control. 'Still, I have to keep an eye on her, especially if she's under any stress.'

Niamh didn't notice his silence. His attention had lapsed. Against the background of her speech, he was carrying on a battle with common sense, telling him how fortunate he was that it had ended like this. Despite his best efforts, however, scraps of the enchantment he once felt floated in his mind. He stopped at Manresa, where three Jesuit novices were walking up the avenue.

'You'll call out to see us sometime,' she said, and without delaying, reached in and kissed him on the lips.

'Of course I will.'

Through the rear-view mirror he watched her walk away, and knew from the purposeful movements and the slight toss of her hair that, despite the half-invitation, they had been together for the last time.

Sixteen

With less than a week to go before Confirmations, the fever in both schools reached boiling point: a replica of the previous year. Brigid Mulchair and Muredach Hogan watched each other like hawks so that one would not outdo the other before the bishop.

Muredach Hogan had got Brannigan's permission to festoon the walls of the church with artwork, supposedly done by the pupils, but mostly the work of a young teacher who had a flair for drawing. The captions glittered in tinfoil: Come Holy Spirit, Love, Peace and Joy, and above all, Holy Trinity Welcomes Our Bishop.

The day before the ceremony, the Confirmation classes assembled for the final rehearsal. The two principals greeted each other with smiles and, as always in public, a double handshake. They knelt together in front of the altar in silent prayer, then proceeded to outrival one another as they simpered and pirouetted around the sanctuary. Brigid Mulchair commanded the lectern microphone and issued instructions to the children about the seating arrangements. In front of the altar, Dick Hegarty sat in the episcopal chair and, to the side, Hogan fidgeted with sheets of paper and whispered every so often to one of his teachers. If he noticed someone talking or sniggering, he broke off his conversation and clicked his fingers in the child's face.

Before they rehearsed the rite of Confirmation, a whispered disagreement commenced between the two principals about the way the children should approach the bishop. The hissing exchange could be heard all over the church, until Dick rushed over and turned off the microphone. Children began to look around and giggle.

'*Ciúnas*,' shrieked Brigid Mulchair. 'I said *ciúnas!*' She glared at the teachers, who made a show of looking around for culprits, but exchanged roguish looks when the principal resumed her instruction.

The outer door slammed shut and every head turned to the side where a key scraped in the lock. In an instant, Miss Mulchair's clouded look became a broad smile for the parish priest.

'Getting on fine, Father,' carried over the microphone as he approached the altar. Like a shame-faced schoolboy, Dick vacated the bishop's chair. Brian had seen the same performance the year before and knew what was to follow. He eased open the front door and escaped into the sunlight.

While he was walking up and down in front of the church, the full swell of the organ and the choir singing 'We are One in the Spirit' reached him. He smiled, recalling the scene he had just witnessed, especially the self-satisfied gait of the parish priest when he took over the bishop's chair: a sixty-two-year-old adolescent sniffing at a fantasy.

Other parishes were no different: they too had their Brigid Mulchairs and their Leo Brannigans, who filled their days, purring with the satisfaction that they were handing on the faith. The phantom nudged him again: did he want to spend the rest of his life playing a supporting role in this absurd drama?

Other elements of the farce came to him: Looby strutting around Lourdes with the diocesan pilgrimage, inquiring of old people if they had slept well the night before; Lynsky seeking invitations to lunch with those who wielded power. Like others before him, he could, in time, expect what he craved: a call to the inner circle. The pointy hat and the gold ring would then be within his grasp.

While all this distanced Brian from the herd, the outsider's view no longer alarmed him. Instead, he saw gates opening to a new horizon, whatever decision lay beyond.

He rose early on the morning of Confirmation and crossed by the laurel hedge to open the church. From the top of Greenoaks Lawn came the clink of milk bottles, an electric motor whined, side mirrors glinted in the sunlight. After breakfast, while waiting for the newsagent to open, he examined the rose bushes, then he pushed open the wooden gate that led to the back garden. The air in the greenhouse was dense with the wholesome smell of earth; green buds were already shooting from the tomato plants. Soon he would have to tie them to the roof so that in August when they ripened, they would bear the weight. On a shelf, the geraniums his mother had put in the car boot on a visit home were ablaze with colour.

He brought his breviary from the house and read Morning Prayer sitting on the garden seat that faced the sun. Halfway up the far wall Virginia creepers clung to the trellis; at one corner sprigs of heather grew between the pile of rocks and, by the garden shed, fuchsia bells like earrings drooped over the blackened skillet.

In the crowded church grounds after Confirmation, the parents all agreed that the ceremony was beautiful and not at all like their days when parents were locked out. They called Brian to stand for photographs while they were waiting for the bishop. 'All the same, you'd have to hand it to Mr Hogan and Miss Mulchair,' they said; 'they do great work with the kiddies, Father.'

'Great work.'

He collected the Mass booklets, strewn on the benches or thrown open on the floor, and placed them in neat bundles on a table beside the baptismal font. Then he knelt for a few moments at the front seat where the smell of incense still lingered. Smoke curled upwards from the candles and dissipated in the air when the altar boy lifted the metal cone of the extinguisher.

'Will I put out the missalettes for the evening Mass, Father?' Radiant after telling the bishop about his vocation, the head altar boy was at his shoulder.

'Do please, Xavier. Thanks.'

The altar boy's happy footsteps receded towards the sacristy door.

As soon as the bishop had gone, Brian rang Brookfield. Since Margaret was off to Paris on Thursday, he wondered whether they might meet the following day. He was on the early Masses, so they could drive to Wicklow and have lunch at that place she liked in Delgany.

'I was going to suggest we meet anyway, because from Monday I will spend a few days on retreat in Manresa.'

'Around twelve then.'

The two postulants, Frances and Stephanie, were pushing their bicycles out of the shed when he pulled up at the privet hedge the following day. They waved and Margaret's words came back to him. 'By the way things are going, probably our last two, *in saecula saeculorum.*'

Frances had worked with the Electricity Supply Board for twenty years, and lived on her own beside Dundrum library. Every Friday evening she used to take out two books for the weekend. She was even thinner than the last time he'd seen her: now the white blouse hung slack around her.

Stephanie blushed and adjusted the bridge of her glasses. They were making the most of the fine weather, she said; the previous day they had cycled as far as the Papal Cross in the Phoenix Park.

'Look, I'm as red as a lobster,' Frances extended her arm for inspection. 'But I don't think I'll die this time, do you, Brian?'

Stephanie pulled up the sleeve of her cardigan and held a milky limb beside the lobster: the contrast caused more laughter. As always, Frances secured centre stage. Through the haze of high spirits, Brian saw her: a little girl still seeking the attention she should have received when she had been farmed out to a childless aunt and uncle. The thin-lipped woman, her mother, could no longer endure her husband's drinking, so she left her cashier's job in the Home and Colonial, and joined her sister in Philadelphia.

He rang the bell and waited at the oak door. At the foot of the sloping lawn, the magnificent cedar of Lebanon brought to mind whitewashed houses of the East; a stream of heat danced between the row of poplars down by the river. To his left, two straight lines of white lawn blocks at each side of the gravel path led the eye to a temple where the Virgin Mary, with hands joined, was contemplating heaven.

After lunch in the Delgany Inn, he drove towards Greystones, careful to avoid cyclists who were laughing and veering in and out on the narrow winding road. When they reached a hilltop beyond the town, Margaret pointed to a Georgian house, half-hidden in the trees. A long line of white fencing defined the driveway that led to the main door. 'That was ours once; where we spent the summer holidays. It was a dower house before we got it: some landlord's present to his daughter on her wedding day.'

'Who lives there now?'

She mentioned a well-known television personality.

'A sign of the times. The religious bought from the gentry and now the TV stars and pop singers are buying from the congregations.'

'We're the Last of the Mohicans, Margaret. Only four ordinations this year in All Saints.'

He drove on until he found a spot that afforded a view right down to the sea.

'That cove was our private beach. There's a path leading off from the driveway. Look, the route we took when we went for our swim.'

In his mind, he saw the procession of young women in cream habits slinking along by the hawthorn hedge; suppression of youthful exuberance when they had to raise their long skirts to avoid a cowpat or sticklebacks.

'And did you torment the local farmers by getting into swim-suits?'

She laughed at the absurdity. 'We were so far away, we couldn't torment anyone. Stanislaus, the mistress of novices, saw to that. Anyway the swimsuit covered as much as the habit.'

At the village, he turned left onto the coast road, a by-way barely the width of two cars. Around the entrance to the strand clusters of people lay between the rocks. Some had erected striped windbreakers; at the sea's edge, children shrieked when the tide ran over their legs and tugged at the gravel underfoot.

'Let's head for a quieter spot, down that way.' He pointed in the direction of the rough path separating the strand from the railway track. When the radios and screams of children were out of range, they set the deckchairs in a hollow screened by sand dunes. He handed her the sun lotion and sank into the chair with an exaggerated sigh of contentment. From her bag she took a paperback and a pair of sunglasses.

They read in a comfortable silence, broken only by the rustle of a page or the whistle of the sea breeze through the reeds above their heads. He grew drowsy and let his newspaper fall over his chest. Drifting off, he was conscious of the surge and break of the tide and the crunch of the beach pebbles dragged outwards by the receding waves. The bottle of wine they had shared over lunch had made him sleepy and, dozing off, he felt the sun through his light slacks, and had a vague sense of arousal.

She was still reading when he woke. She sat cross-legged, one sandal hanging by its toestrap; beneath the white blouse, shoulder straps strained against rounded flesh.

Aware of his inspection, she inserted the marker and closed the book. 'Why the stare?' she asked, placing the sunglasses on her head.

' "The cat may look at the queen," we used to say in my part of the country.'

'Strange cats in your part of the country, I imagine.'

The suntan oil had dried and he applied more to his face and arms, filling the air with a rich scent of coconut.

'There,' he held the bottle towards her. 'I wouldn't have it on my conscience if you got sunburn.'

From the direction of the strand entrance, 'Greensleeves' rang out and brought whoops of excitement from the children: through the swaying reeds he watched them dash for the ice cream van.

Margaret had unbuttoned the top part of her blouse and was struggling to reach over her shoulder.

'I'll do that for you,' he offered, and, at once, was kneeling behind her chair. She surrendered the bottle. The blissful feel of her skin, the curve of the breasts above the white brassiere set his imagination ablaze.

As if he had her under a spell, she offered no resistance. He removed her sunglasses, drew her down on the grassy floor and kissed her slowly and deliberately. Through the summer clothes, every contour was accessible to his touch. The sweeping movement caused her skirt to rise above her knee.

It was then she stiffened, and recoiled from his embrace. She sat up, pulled the skirt over her legs and entwined her hands about her knees in a protective manner. 'No,' she said, avoiding his eyes. 'It's not that I wouldn't want to go further.' She kept looking out at the sea. 'And you're the only one I would ever say that to. It's just that it would be all wrong – I don't mean the sexual aspect.'

'What do you mean?'

'It would probably ruin what is between us. I've known too many relationships between people in our situation that were spoiled by going too far.'

'But it's only natural.'

'Yes, natural. That seems to give a licence to everything. You know Angela that teaches with me?'

A mental image of the spindle-thin, eager-to-please nun came to him.

'She had a friend in the diocese; they met at one of those Encounter Retreats. When he was down in Wicklow, she visited him on weekends, supposedly to wash his curtains or do a clean up of his house. It had become a joke with us: "Are you off to do the curtains, Angie?" That went on for years until he was transferred to a city parish and he said Mass in one of our convents. Very soon he was inseparable from another nun whom I won't name because she is well-known as a spiritual director.'

'So I might sell you down the river.'

'That is not my fear and you know it' was delivered with the same determination that had cut short his fervour. It wasn't the first time she had shown such iron resolve, a reaction that frustrated him, and one at variance with the open door of her friendliness.

In frustration, he turned away, tore a blade of grass from the ground and flung it to the wind. 'That's not morality,' he snapped. 'That's putting a lid on life, the result of conditioning and traipsing down to the sea hidden from everyone. I mean....' He tried to take the sting out.

'No. Maybe you're right about putting a lid on. And I know also that I am, if you like, planted in an institution. That is my decision. I suppose if I trotted off to a counsellor or took one of those renewal courses in Chicago, I might return to Brookfield, as they say, "in touch with all my feelings". Devouring poor old nuns if they crossed me because I had been told to express my anger. I might even find out that my adolescence was foreclosed or that I've an unconscious distrust of men, picked up from Mother.'

She was close to tears, but she braced herself.

'I'm staying where I am, and I'm not getting involved with you in a way that you might want. I'll be your friend, but that's the limit.' She rested her head on her crouched up knees and stared at the ground.

After some time he picked up her sunglasses that lay on the sand, took out a handkerchief and slowly wiped the lenses. 'There,' he said, settling them on her head. Grinning, he leaned towards her. 'I take it you don't want any more suntan lotion then.'

Some time during the night he woke to a rumble that sounded like the explosion of heavy artillery. Then came a flash of lightning followed by a prolonged crash of thunder. It continued to rend the air, so loud that it could tear the house apart. Sleep became impossible. He heard the first plop of raindrops quickly merging into a continuous dull thud on the tiled roof. The flashes lit up the dark wood of the wardrobe, the chest of drawers and the crucifix, so that the scene resembled a set from an old black and white film.

Unable to sleep, he played over in his mind the incident at the strand. He had to admit that the intimacies he sought could never happen between him and Margaret, and once again he came face to face with the unavoidable question – why not leave now, meet someone who wasn't bound by vows or ensnared to the past? He gave free rein to the fantasy: he was still young enough and his honours degree would enable him to do postgraduate studies. For a week or two he'd be the talking point at Royal Dublin: What's he doing? Is there a woman? How did his mother take it? He turned away from the flashing lights on the curtains. Yes, his mother would meet the setback with the same steely smile she wore for the world throughout her life. Whenever they talked about Paul's leaving, her throwaway comment seemed to have a wider application: 'I'd prefer to see him content than living a life of misery.'

As when a child, he began to count the seconds between the lightning and thunder; gradually the gap widened. The rumble ceased but the rain rilled down the tiles, along the eaves and spilled through the drain cover. A wild notion to go out and stand beneath the downpour flashed across his mind and he smiled at the absurdity. He imagined Dick, next door, calling Dympna to see the madman. He grew drowsy again and eased into sleep, and for the first time in his life, savoured the delicious taste of freedom to make a choice about his future.

He woke to the slow drip from the drainpipes. Unlike his usual cereal and toast, he had a leisurely breakfast of grilled bacon and scrambled egg. Over coffee he glanced through the curriculum vitae and references of the candidates Muredach Hogan had shortlisted for a vacant post. In the afternoon both of them would interview in his front room.

Before Miss Cummiskey and the Rosary Brigade arrived in the church, he had nearly an hour's peace. The year had come full circle again: after Wednesday all would be quiet around the school. Margaret would be gone and he had a whole summer to mull over the promises he had made when he lay prostrate on the cold marble of All Saints Chapel.

Of this he was certain: the mysterious appeal that drew him to that sanctuary still called, except that now he knew the price to pay if he continued to answer. The pull still surprised him at unexpected moments: over a sea of flickering candles on an

Easter Saturday night; on Christmas Eve when the last of the penitents had left; and during the period before midnight Mass when he walked in the midst of hushed, expectant streets.

At such times, he glimpsed his dream as new and fresh as the first time he nodded to its whisper.

Images floated before him: the boy standing at the corner of Melrose Avenue who offered him the packet of crisps; Phyllis Jordan's efforts to make something out of the place; his old friend, Tim Sheridan, who brought the ESB to the Wicklow hills and his words that evening in Dún Laoghaire: 'The Church needs men like you.'

Over the summer, he would make the most important decision of his life, he reflected calmly.

That evening in the sacristy he prepared a pre-nuptial inquiry form. 'Will you do the wedding, Father Brian?' the young woman asked.

He stopped writing and raised his head. 'When are you getting married?'

'The twelfth of November.'

Taken unawares, he gave the best excuse he could invent: 'I can't promise you now because in the meantime I could be changed to another parish. We never know in my job. I will let you know at the end of August if that's any good.'

'The end of August will be fine.'

When she had gone, he entered the wedding date in the parish diary. In the silence he picked up the voices of the other two priests coming from the office. The tone was friendly and relaxed: two men marching after the same drummer. At times Dick Hegarty grew animated; he seemed to be calling the attention of the parish priest to what he had missed.

Brian was about to file the marriage papers in the grey cabinet when the other curate put his head inside the door and looked around. 'Your woman is gone. Good. Come in for a minute.' He indicated towards the office and threw his eyes heavenwards.

Seated at the table was the parish priest, who was examining from different angles what looked like an empty fish tank with a tube inside. 'Watch this,' he said and pressed a switch at the side.

A light came on and the machine stirred into life. The tube coughed out table tennis balls with numbers on them. They rolled along a channel at the top and came to rest. Over the whine of the motor, Father Brannigan gave a commentary: 'It's a godsend. Imagine all the bother it will save us at the bingo every Thursday night.' The three priests stood and followed the flow of the balls from the mouth of the funnel. 'And the great thing about it is you can regulate the movement. Look.' The parish priest turned another switch and the flow slackened. 'One of my ordination class told me about it at the retreat.' He laid a proprietary hand on top as he looked fondly at the machine.

'Great isn't it?' Dick sustained the momentum.

'Wonderful,' Brian replied with the right measure of conviction. For a respectful length of time, he contributed scraps to the purr from the other two priests about how it would be a major asset to the parish. Then he excused himself, muttering about having to set in order the marriage papers. His leaving went unnoticed. At the door he glanced back at the flickering play on the faces of the priests: two boys at a toy-shop window.

Like someone in two minds about his next move, he stood on the step outside the church. Perched on the wooden cross near the road, a bird flapped its wings, soared to a great height and glided across the freshly washed sky. From one of the flats in Davis Towers a woman leaned over the balcony and screamed at children who were playing down below on the concrete.

It was quiet across in Holy Trinity, much quieter than the day Father Brannigan had brought his new curate to see the Church of the Resurrection. In the courtyard of the school, Brian unzipped the black cover of his breviary, blessed himself and read the final prayer of the day.

AFTERWORD

Some years ago, the highly acclaimed American psychologist and academic, Eugene Kennedy, conducted a survey of attitudes among Roman Catholic priests in the United States. Broadly speaking, he found that a majority were no less happy than those in other professions. Most likely he would have come up with the same result in Ireland.

But that was 1970, before a tsunami battered the Catholic Church. The social status accorded to clerics and religious in those days is now history. Once upon a time in Ireland, the priest headed every committee in his parish: he could pick up the phone and appoint a teacher whom he knew 'has a solid faith' to the post of principal of the local Catholic school; rows of penitents knelt outside his confessional on a Saturday night. Regrettably, they didn't always meet with the compassion of the kindly old priest in Patrick Kavanagh's poem 'Father Matt' whose voice 'rises and falls like a briar in the breeze'.

I was among a group of priests who were ordained in the early seventies. We were young, idealistic and eager to shatter the image of the staid generation of priests who had gone before us. We would be among the first out on the dance floor at wedding receptions. We wore jeans, long hair (oh happy days!) and played guitars. We came 'trailing clouds of glory' – or so we thought. In hindsight, we were decidedly naive.

On weekends away on retreats with the youth club, teenagers called us by our first name. We sat around on bean bags and shared our inner world. In the barque of Peter we were enjoying 'fair winds and following seas'. One bishop advised us to have the documents of the Ecumenical Council in one hand and the ESRI report in the other. The world is a good place, Vatican II announced.

Over time, however, like a door knob in constant use, the gloss began to wear off. The demands of the sacrifice began to be felt. Things fell apart. Some of our colleagues could no longer endure the isolation of coming home to a presbytery emptier than empty. We went to their weddings, made generous speeches about how 'Michael will bring to his marriage the depth of humanity he brought to the priesthood.' We sang at the reception and we drove back through the night with images of our colleague and his bride cutting the cake and leading the dance floor for the opening set.

As the years progressed, the hopes for Vatican II also were eroded. Archbishop John Charles McQuaid of Dublin returned from the Council to assure his flock that 'no change will worry the tranquillity of your Christian lives'.

Slowly but surely, we were experiencing what F. Scott Fitzgerald described as 'a thinning brief-case of enthusiasm'. A bishop fathers a child; another bishop absconds with his housekeeper. But much more was to follow: tragic events that would shock the Catholic world. The fissures in the beautiful mosaic were now widening. Calls for an end to mandatory celibacy fell on deaf ears. Many continued to find fulfilment in the ministry, but others were now living Thoreau's 'lives of quiet desperation'. *The Strangled Impulse* is an attempt to render that darkness at the heart of the priesthood.

The phone calls and letters, from priests and laity, the media interest I received when the novel hit the bookshops convinced me that I had aired truths about the condition of priests at that time in Ireland. For some weeks the book was a best-seller, second only to Seamus Heaney's *The Haw Lantern*. I would settle to be pipped to the post by Heaney any day.

There was some criticism also from the ranks: 'Bad enough for the media to be doing this to us, but one of our own!' I took some comfort in Cardinal Suhard's comment: 'One of the priest's first services to the world is to tell the truth.'

The Strangled Impulse is a fictionalized account of priests who were ordained in the late nineteen sixties and early seventies: young men who left the seminary, ready to go 'where angels fear to tread', at a time when churches were full; young people were swarming to the youth Mass in Rathmines and elsewhere. They gave their time to summer camps and clubs; they did retreats with the Jesuits at Tabor House. John Paul II's visit to the Phoenix Park attracted a sea of saffron and white in 'an apple-ripe September morn'. The world was young; we would never die. Eden before the Fall.

A bit like the Wild Geese, some of our confrères left with their wives or partners to places like Britain or the United States; those who remained – many who are as fulfilled as anyone can expect to be – continue as priests, following as best they can the dream born in the shepherd's hut.